YOU ARE HERE

Geonn Cannon

Supposed Crimes LLC • Matthews, North Carolina

ISBN: 978-1-952150-49-4

www.supposedcrimes.com

This book is typeset in Goudy Old Style.

YOU ARE HERE

IN THE DARK, Vera was awake. Vera was aware.

The forward section of the living space was home to a command center. A captain's chair facing a ring of green screens and keyboards backlit with a gentle blue glow. The overhead lights were off, the darkness tinted teal from the blended light of the controls.

An egg-shaped sarcophagus lay length-wise behind the command center. A woman lay within the shell, her arms floating by her sides, her face covered by a full mask which fed her oxygen, nutrients, and meds which ensured she remained unconscious. A visor over her sleeping eyes fed her dream scenarios to keep her mind active in its long slumber. Monitors attached to the woman's wrists, chest, and temple let Vera know when the captain was scared, frightened, excited. She knew every beat of the woman's heart and the tempo of her breathing.

While the captain slept, the ship passed through dangers both visible and unseen. Tiny projectiles hurtling at unbelievable speed. Thick bands of radiation that tested the limits of the ship's shielding. Vera took care of each threat without strain or stress, calculating vectors that would avoid red zones and keep them more or less on their scheduled path.

On the exterior, hundreds of cameras mapped where they were going, what was around them, and where they had been, sending exabytes of information to computers on the ship that translated the information into a map that was transmitted back home every ten hours.

Vera was everywhere within the ship. Her attention could be narrowed to a pinpoint, or expanded to cover everything at once.

Like now, when a screen on the command console lit up, flickered in the darkness, and then filled with information. Vera's focus was drawn to this readout by an alert.

An intriguing alert.

An alert which required her captain's immediate attention.

CHAPTER ONE

XARI YACINE was currently a knight, returning from a valiant quest to slay a dragon.

Or... maybe she was a Viking? She looked down at her body. She saw chainmail, covered by a breastplate of iron pieces welded together. Dents and dings and scratches covered the armor but she didn't see any blood or feel any wounds. The design itself didn't tell her which story she was in. She had a sword. Vikings didn't carry swords, did they? No helmet, but the horned helmet legend was bullshit anyway. For the time being, she decided to run with the idea she was a knight. She'd just slain a dragon, after all. Vikings didn't do that.

She was in a wide green field that sloped at a steep angle down to a vicious cliff overlooking the brightest blue sea she'd ever seen. A blonde woman stood on the precipice, staring out toward the horizon. Her hair was twisted into twin braids that met at the base of her skull and continued down into a long rope that reached to her waist.

Xari rested her hand on the hilt of her sword. She smiled and started walking. Now she was certain what story this was.

The blonde turned as Xari approached. The woman's face split into a wide smile, and she ran to meet her halfway. They met with a powerful collision, the frail woman hitting the iron breastplate with enough force that it must have knocked the wind out of her. She didn't seem to notice or care. Xari squeezed her tightly, then stepped back and examined her face. The wind blew loose strands of hair into her face. Xari brushed them away, the material of her gloves rough against the impossibly smooth skin. She knew the woman's name as soon as she saw her face.

"Linnea, my love."

"You're back!" her wife said, gasping the words. "My brave knight."

"Was there ever any doubt?" Xari said, the Viking confusion fading. "A dragon is no match for one who has someone like you waiting at home."

Linnea narrowed her eyes. "Your words are sweeter than your kisses, and even more distracting. What are you hiding, my knight?"

"From you? Nothing, ever." She put her arms around Linnea, fingers laced in the small of her back. "But perhaps I am a crafty knight who requires intense interrogation."

"Are you the sort to buckle under torture?"

Xari tilted her head to one side. "It would depend on the talents of the torturer."

Linnea slipped her right hand under Xari's armor, lifting the chainmail to touch skin. "I've had no complaints. But I have perhaps lost my touch while you were away. We~" Her eyes cut to the left, over Xari's shoulder. "As much as I crave your presence, my knight, I am afraid your companion requires your attention."

"My...?"

Xari turned to see a tall woman in a white jumpsuit, her hair pinned in a way that allowed red curls to fall across both shoulders. Her arms were clasped behind her back, her head tilted toward the sky to observe the clouds, an affectation of giving Xari privacy that annoyed more than anything else.

She pressed her lips together, frustrated, and reluctantly stepped away from Linnea's embrace. "Vera. I thought I requested privacy."

"You did, Captain." Vera took a step forward. "I apologize for the intrusion. But my command protocols override any personal directives you've set."

Xari sighed and faced Linnea again. "It looks like my homecoming will have to wait for another day, my sweet." She kissed Linnea's forehead, then turned away from her. She walked to where Vera was waiting. "You couldn't have waited fifteen minutes?"

"Again, apologies. My command~"

"Command protocols are very strict, I know, I know." Xari sighed and closed her eyes. "Okay. Give me two minutes."

Vera said, "I will be waiting."

Xari inhaled deeply and let the air out slowly. The armor was the first to vanish, followed by the waves crashing at the base of the cliff going silent. Gravity shifted ever so slightly. Her body acquired weight, actual weight. The liquid in which she'd been floating drained away and gently deposited her onto a soft mattress molded into the shape of her body. She only became aware of a clamped pressure around her face when it was release, and a mask was lifted. She stretched and flexed her fingers and gave a soft grunt, cleared her throat, coughed softly.

Finally she opened her eyes. The shell of her pod opened, and she carefully lifted herself up and out. The wires and tubes that had connected her to the ship systems and virtual reality feed had disconnected as she woke. They trailed behind her as she emerged, and the glass cover slid back in place once she was out. Now she was wearing a skintight gray uniform with sleeves that ended just below the elbow, pants that ended at the knee. She was barefoot, but she didn't bother looking for her boots.

"Danger level?" Her brain was still struggling to adjust to the reality of her ship, of who she was. Where she was. No dragon-slaying knight, certainly no Viking, but an explorer and adventurer nonetheless.

"Minimal, Captain." Vera's response came from a single speaker mounted in the arm rest of the captain's chair. She'd originally been programmed to use every speaker at once, but Xari had changed that her first day aboard. She wanted the ship's artificial intelligence to sound like someone she was speaking to, not an omnipresent God voice.

Xari settled into the seat. "How long has it been since I was last awake?"

"Seventeen weeks and four days," Vera said.

"Long nap," Xari said. "Nice dreams."

Vera said, "I am glad to hear that, Captain."

She scanned the screens that spread out on the command panel in front of her, taking in the information without truly reading it. "If the threat is minimal, then that means you must have some exciting news for me."

"Potentially." A screen lit up next to Xari's left hand. She read the information as Vera reported what it said. "I've located a planet with the appropriate size and distance from the sun to prove viable for settlement. Standard checks have come back positively, so I woke you to confirm the readings before a report is sent back to the colony ships."

"You needed the human touch, hm?" Xari tapped the readout and opened a scan of the planet in question. "Time to earn my paycheck, I guess. How far away are we from the planet?"

"With a slight course correction, we can arrive in just under two days. I have determined the proper bearing and will engage at your command."

"So you woke me up because you needed authorization?" She raised an eyebrow. "I gave you more leeway than that."

"Normally, I would have done so, as per your orders. But this required a more nuanced examination."

"I'm intrigued. So let's see what we have here." She skimmed the readout, which showed a scan of a dark planet wrapped in swirling clouds. "Pretty little planet. Orbiting in the habitable zone of a red dwarf. Indications of surface water, nice. Signs of..." Her voice trailed off and she narrowed her eyes as she re-read the information.

Vera interpreted the silence correctly. "That also gave me pause. Signs of civilization. No artificial satellites and a lack of large cities, but we're close enough for our scans to reveal a network of roads and what appear to be irrigation and other signs of an agrarian society. Shall I set us on course to take a closer look?"

"Hold your horses," Xari said. "Let's be sure it's worth the time and effort to get there. An existing society would disqualify it as a potential new home. But... we could just swing by. See if there's enough room for maybe *one* colony. Maybe they'd be willing to share their planet with some refugees. Nothing says we all have to end up on the same planet, right?"

Vera said, "That was not in the charter, no."

"Not to mention..." She gave an excited laugh. "First contact."

"First contact with a wholly alien species," Vera said.

Xari took a deep breath, then glanced at the screen. "Unless..."

"No other Seeker ships have reported a similar discovery."

"Then... we might make history."

Vera said, "It would be very exciting."

"Of course not. Would you like music while you examine the readings?"

Xari said, "Yeah. DJ's choice."

"As you wish."

Medieval music started playing from speakers all around her. Xari smiled and shook her head, smirking at the AI's choice

"Maybe chivalry isn't dead after all."

"Perhaps not, Captain."

Despite the fact it should've been impossible, Xari definitely detected a trace of laughter in the AI's voice.

The purpose of the Astraea Seeker Project was simple. Humanity needed to expand to other planets if they hoped to survive another generation. Scientists had discovered a number of potential new homes, but warned it would be impossible to know for certain how viable they were for colonization without up-close exploration. The amount of power required to move an entire colony ship to just one of the planets was astronomical. They couldn't afford the gamble of choosing one and spending all their resources on a planet that might not be suitable.

Fortunately there was a solution. Smaller one-person ships outfitted with an Eckles-Sullivan engine could travel further, faster, and cheaper.

All of this was explained to Xari in the office of the Astraea Human Resources Southwestern Region Representative. She had passed every exam, all the screening processes, the rigorous training that bordered on torture, and now only one step remained: the HR rep needed to be sure she understood the gravity of her responsibility before he cleared her for assignment.

He was an average man in every respect. Average height, medium attractiveness, bald, with a wide jaw and small eyes. He spoke with an accent so vague that she could only narrow it down to "New York" but even that was a shot in the dark. He leaned back in his chair and examined her carefully. He held a pencil in one hand, lightly thumping it against the palm of the other like a metronome clicking.

She sat across from him in her uncomfortable green jumpsuit. Regulations required it had to be buttoned to the throat. It felt like she was being choked by it.

"There's a very real chance you'll never be able to return to Earth," he said, watching her carefully for any facial reaction to this announcement. "If anything goes wrong with your ship, if your power supply fails, you'll be stranded outside the reach of any rescue. Are you clear about that?"

"It was made exceedingly clear, sir," she said. "I've accepted the possibility."

He leaned forward and rested his elbows on the desk. "Why?"

She returned his stare. "I was told I wouldn't be required to give a reason."

"You're not." His demeanor had changed. He was more relaxed now, less bureaucrat and more human. They might have still been on the record, but she knew that this wasn't an official query. "But if we're going to put all these resources behind your candidacy, I'd kind of like to know why you're willing to climb into a tin can there's a very good chance you'll never climb out of again. Seeker ships are cheaper than sending a colony ship, but we still can't afford to hand one over to someone who might just fly it into the sun."

Xari relaxed. She folded her hands in her lap.

"My wife died. It was a slow death. We saw it coming, but of course that didn't make any of it easier. She spent a long time fighting and then one day it... was over. For a little while, I told myself I was just feeling grief. There's no timeline for grief, right? So. It didn't matter that it lasted for a year. Two years was a little suspect. But when three years had gone by..."

The commander nodded slowly.

"It's been six years," Xari said. "I don't feel the... I'm past the dark days. The days when people would come over to make sure I'd fed and bathed myself and all that. But every day... every day is just the same. More of the same. Just emptiness, and pointless, like I'm just waiting for it all to end. I figure, um, that if I'm just killing time until everything ends, I might as well be doing something that helps others. And this project will help all of humanity. So. That's worthy. And I think it's something Linnea would be proud of."

"That's your wife's name?" he said.

Xari nodded. "Yeah."

The commander sat up straight and put down the pencil. He glanced toward her file and gave a short, quick nod.

"Okay, then. You passed all the qualifying exams with flying colors. You might not be the best candidate in some individual categories, but you're far enough to the head of the pack that your overall score gets you just over the finish line."

Xari breathed out a sigh of relief and nodded. "Thank you." She stood up and extended her hand.

The commander took it, squeezed. "Given the mission, it seems a little self-serving to wish you good luck. But I'm going to do it anyway. Godspeed, Captain Yasine."

"Thank you, sir."

She left Earth six months later. On the ride to the launchpad from the barracks where she'd been quarantined, she felt like she should feel melancholy. She watched the fields roll by out the window, tilted her head back to look at the shapes the clouds made. And yes, it was sad that she might never see another sunny day. But neither would Linnea. And Xari hadn't truly appreciated the sky since she died, so it wasn't like she was sacrificing anything. She'd already sacrificed the beauty in the world, or it had sacrificed her. She could appreciate the beauty of the world but she couldn't make herself give a shit about it.

There were seven Seeker ships in the fleet. Hers was the first to launch since she was the first captain to clear all the background and psychological checks. She was allowed to choose the name, since it was going to be her home for the foreseeable future. She chose the *Canary*, after a classic rock band, and also because she felt like a canary in a coal mine. Heading off into the darkness to find safe places for the rest of humanity to follow.

It was already on the runway in preparation for the launch when she arrived. The ship would take off like a plane, controlled by the onboard artificial intelligence to assure everything went perfectly. Xari was a qualified pilot, but the people in charge didn't want to take any chances on this inaugural launch. She was assured there would be no issues, everything would go smoothly, all the test flights and simulations had gone off without a hitch.

The ship was the first thing she saw when they arrived at the spaceport. She sat up, truly taking notice of something for the first time since leaving the barracks. The *Canary* was the size of a city block and shaped like a bird of prey, head down, wings arched and extended. The cockpit was in the bird's head, the brain center, while her living space was in the central body of the vessel. Everything else either helped the ship run or stored things to keep her alive. It looked immense compared to the landscape around it, but she knew how tiny it would feel once it was just her and the ship in the vastness of space.

She was delivered onboard by a group of men and women in white lab uniforms, glasses, respirator masks so they wouldn't give her any last-minute illness. Her suit was sprayed down for the same reason. Her vitals were checked one last time. When the all-clear was given, the hatch was sealed behind her. Xari removed her mask and took her first breath of filtered air, looking around her new home. Her entire world, actually.

It was a single room, command chair and stasis chamber in the center, with multipurpose areas along the back walls. It had been carefully designed to be comfortable while still taking up the least amount of space possible. Benches and tables folded up into walls, container units were everywhere she looked. She still had to look over the inventory to remember where everything was, but she was sure she'd have it figured out in no time.

Xari strapped herself into the command chair and sent the all-clear to Ground Control. She took a deep breath and curled her fingers around the armrests. A honeycombed viewscreen took up most of the wall in front of her. It was designed to look like a window, but it was a series of screens displaying live readouts of the area directly in front of the ship. When not in use, the honeycomb could be closed to leave a smooth expanse of white that wouldn't distract her from the command panel. But for now, it was open and active, and she could see the runway stretching out ahead of them, and above it... open sky.

She remembered the AI. It should have already been online, so she cleared her throat. "Vera?"

"Hello, Captain Yacine. How may I assist you?"

The voice came directly from speakers in her helmet. "Am I distracting you?"

"I'm incapable of distraction, Captain."

Xari nodded. "Okay, then. Um. I'd like something to distract *me* from what's about to happen. You have a music library, right?"

"Correct. It was curated from your selected preferences. Would you like me to play an album at random, or is there a specific artist you'd like to hear?"

Xari licked her lips, then smiled. "Give me some *Space Oddity*. The 2009 remaster."

"An appropriate choice, Captain."

"Wait until the countdown is at one minute and twenty-two seconds before you start it."

Vera said, "Is there a particular reason for this choice?"

Xari smiled. Possibly her first sincere smile in over six years. "Just something I've wanted to do since I signed up for this."

"As you wish, Captain Yacine."

There was a long silence from the speakers, filled with the sounds of hoses and tubes disengaging the ship from the platform. She felt a rumble through her boots and she wondered if she had gotten the timing wrong. The vibration passed through her chair and into her body, thrumming so loudly she was worried she wouldn't hear the music when it began.

Then she heard it. The song slowly built, a strumming guitar and quiet drum beat mixing with the hum of her engines powering up. The ship surged forward. Bowie sang an extended countdown, going from ten to one in sixteen seconds as she raced along the runaway. The music built to a crescendo and then, at the exact moment her wheels left the ground, the song surged into the triumphant chorus.

The sync was so perfect that Xari let out an unexpected whoop, banged her fist into the arm of her seat, and laughed as the clouds whipped past the viewscreen. Xari could feel the music in her blood, humming across her bones. Blue faded into purple, velvet, then a deep black. The ship gained speed and she sank deeper into the cushions of her chair, pressed back by gravity that she'd soon be free of, and the classic song continued playing in her ears, the perfect soundtrack for leaving Earth for the unknown.

"Thank you, Vera." Xari's voice was breathless and tinged with tears and laughter.

"I am pleased you approve, Captain." Vera sounded as calm as a GPS guiding you to the local supermarket. "The music made the event quite momentous."

Xari grinned, surprised to discover there were tears in her eyes. Tears of joy and ecstasy, a human reaction to seeing something so unbelievable. She knew hundreds, maybe thousands, of people had been to space but that was still a tiny fraction of humanity. She was a pioneer, one of the first to leave the planet, and she would have known she was dead inside if she didn't have a reaction to that.

"I enjoyed that song very much. Would you like me to add David Bowie to your favored playlist?"

"Yes, I would. I think we're going to get along very well, Vera."

"I am glad, Captain."

Xari smiled and let the end of the song play as they began their long journey.

Chapter Two

Despite the fact Xari was expected to spend the majority of her time either in stasis or the command center, the *Canary* was equipped with all the comforts of a small home. Xari called the ship's living space the Igloo. It was white, with a domed roof, and the walls were ringed with a meal area with a diner-style booth, a small bed where she could have "natural" sleep, a small gym, a "wellness center," and a kitchen. Everything a space explorer needed to feel at home. She knew there was something installed in the floor that created an artificial gravity field, but that was so far outside her area of expertise she didn't even pretend to understand how it worked.

Xari was seated in the booth, her hands folded in front of her on the table. Vera was across from her. The holographic representation of the AI was meant to be used sparingly, preferably only in emergency situations, though no one had ever successfully explained to Xari what sort of emergency would require a virtual crewmember. Xari had only used it a few times, when it felt better to interact with a face than just talking into thin air.

This was one of those times that she considered an emergency.

Vera was a redheaded woman of average height and build. She wore a plain gray jumpsuit that looked exactly like Xari's but was slightly more form-fitting. Xari had often wondered if it *was* her skin. Why bother to create a nude body underneath the clothes? Her posture was perfect, because why wouldn't it be? Her shoulders subtly rose and fell, as if she was breathing, but Xari knew that was just part of the program to make her seem real and not trigger the 'uncanny valley' response in Xari's mind.

It had only been an hour since Vera took her out of stasis. An hour since everything she knew about the universe was turned on its ear. She'd been willing to believe there were planets that could support human life, sure, but planets with life already there? That was science-fiction, that was fantasy, that was Bigfoot and the Tooth Fairy.

But it was real.

The *Canary* was traveling at a greatly diminished speed to remain in proximity to the planet while they debated their options. She could change course for a closer look, or she could increase speed and begin the journey to the next planet in their database. She could declare this world unfit for human colonization and it would be stricken from their records. Or...

Or.

"We can verbally list the pros and cons," Vera said.

Xari shrugged. "It's as good an idea as any. Pro, we could end our mission right now. We send a beacon for the colony ship and call in all the other Seeker ships. Mission accomplished. We start building a new home here so it's ready when the others arrive."

"Con," Vera said, "the native population might not take very kindly to alien invaders."

"That's true. And humanity kind of has a habit of... mm, well."

"Colonization."

Xari nodded. "Right. So maybe it's not worth the effort. Better to keep looking for a place that isn't already claimed."

Vera said, "It would be the path of least resistance in more ways than one."

"Right." Xari drummed her fingers on the table. "Then again... if we look past the purpose of colonizing the planet or finding a new home, we have the opportunity to meet aliens for the first time. Real aliens! The kind that build roads and know about irrigation."

"It would be a pinnacle for all humanity."

Xari grinned. "First man to walk on the Moon, first woman on Mars, and now me. The woman who introduced aliens to humanity." Her smile faded. "Which has the potential of making me a war criminal on their planet, depending on how the rest of humanity reacts when they hear the news. I can't exactly say 'we come in peace' when I have no clue what other countries will do with the information. We could be friendly as anything, cooperate, peaceful. But then maybe the Fel Republic decides they want to just kick us and the natives both out to take it for their own."

Vera raised her eyebrows. "The Fel Republic?"

"Okay, maybe not them," Xari said. "But other nations have the ability to travel this far. And historically we don't really have the most amazing track record with new places. But we can't just ignore this! This is..." She gestured toward the front of the ship. "This is aliens! We discovered *aliens*."

Vera nodded. "Potential. We could be seeing the remnants of a native species which died out long ago."

"True." Xari got excited as she considered that. "But in that case it would be an even better candidate for settling, because there'd already be infrastructure. Even if it *is* just ruins. It's a step above starting from nothing. And it would be proof intelligent life *can* and *has* existed in the universe outside of Earth. That by itself would be monumental."

"The archaeologists would be very excited if that is the case."

"A whole new history to unlock."

Vera nodded. "Exactly."

Xari slumped back against the booth. "Do we have to make an official report about everything I discover on the planet?"

"Not necessarily," Vera said. "The report doesn't have to be comprehensive. It can focus on disqualifying features of the planet without going into detail. If things become dire, the committee might request a more in-depth analysis, but I doubt that will be necessary."

Xari slapped her palms down on the table and nodded. "Okay. We'll go, we'll see what we can find out, and we'll figure out our next steps from there. I think that's the best option."

"I agree, it's best to draw conclusions based on all available evidence. Shall I change course for the planet?"

"Absolutely, Vera."

The hologram nodded and flickered out of sight. Xari started to slide out of the booth, but Vera suddenly reappeared.

"Captain Yacine, are you in distress?"

"What?"

"Your vital signs spiked rather dramatically in the past few minutes. A visual examination reveals you seem to be in good health, but if you're~"

Xari grinned. "I'm excited, Vera. There's a chance we're about to meet aliens. I'm just *excited*."

The concern evaporated from Vera's face. "Oh! I suppose that makes a great deal of sense."

Xari laughed and shook her head. "Enter the new coordinates. I have a lot of work to do if I'm going to be ready for first contact."

"Yes, Captain."

Vera faded again, staying gone this time.

Xari stood and went to the library: a panel from which she could access millions of texts. She activated the screen and chewed her bottom lip as she scanned the archives for the proper titles. There were books, essays, long-winded articles covering every possible problem she might encounter. Mechanical, psychological, physical, anything that might go wrong with one person alone on a ship. She knew there was literature about what to do if she encountered aliens, but she had a feeling it had been added as an afterthought. The human race had long ago accepted they were most likely alone in the universe. An accident of sentience in a vast, empty universe.

Her hands were shaking as she typed in the information she needed. She laughed at herself, shook her head, and downloaded the relevant information to her tablet.

Whatever happened on this planet, she was going to make history.

Vera scanned the *Canary* from tip to tail every five-point-three seconds. While she processed the results of these scans, she also monitored the current fuel levels, the amount of solar power stored in the batteries that lined the exterior shell of the ship, and the distance to the nearest light source in case they needed a refill. These calculations played out at the same time she monitored their flightpath to the planet their sensors had picked up, making sure there was nothing to impede their journey.

Vera was always cognizant of where the captain was aboard the ship, if she was healthy or in distress. With the rest of the ship taken care of, Vera focused her attention on the most fragile part of the mission. At the moment, Xari's vital signs indicated she had fallen asleep. It was no surprise; she had been poring over information since their earlier conversation, nearly eighteen hours earlier, reading about hypothetical first contact scenarios.

Xari was sitting at the dinner table, slumped forward with her tablet screen as a pillow. She was in deep sleep, her first true sleep in approximately four months. The rest of the time had been spent in stasis. It was recommended that she spend at least one night every month getting natural rest, but Xari had been lax about that. She had trouble falling and staying asleep on the ship. She would doze off for fifteen minutes, then wake suddenly with some task or chore that needed her attention. It was so much easier to just plug into the machine and spend a few weeks wandering through a perfectly manufactured dream.

Vera was content to let her sleep, even if the position was suboptimal. Her neck and back would be sore when she woke, but it was nothing a bit of stretching and exercise couldn't fix. Her breathing was steady and her sleep was solid. That was the important thing at the moment.

She noticed that it was nearly time for Xari to have another haircut. She normally kept it a little longer on top, with a bit on the sides, but shaved close to the scalp above the ears and at the base of her skull. Much easier to deal with if it was that short. But Vera had access to photos of Xari from the ship's archives and she knew that before, on Earth, she had worn her hair very long. Thick and black and full of curls, she could sweep it forward to hide her face or to peek out from behind the veil. Vera knew it must have been a huge adjustment to go from such a style to something much shorter. It was a matter of weight and convenience, but also she knew that people could have an odd emotional attachment to their hair. Choosing, or being ordered, to cut it all off must have been a strange and emotional experience.

Vera's omnipresent attention told her there was nothing else on the ship that required her attention, so she continued her examination of Xari. She didn't know why she found the captain so fascinating. She could be grumpy after waking from stasis, or waking from natural sleep. She could be stubborn. There had been times when she referred to Vera or the *Canary* as a "stupid piece of shit machine." But she always apologized later. And she had explained to Vera that humans could say things in anger that they didn't mean.

"You're not a stupid machine," she'd said after one such outburst.

"I'm not technically smart, either," Vera admitted. "I simply have access to a vast store of information which I can access in a split second, giving me the impression of intelligence. And you are correct in your assessment that I am a machine."

Xari shook her head and looked toward the ceiling speaker. "No. You're a friend. You're the only one keeping me from going absolutely crazy out here. Can you do me a favor and remember that the next time *I* get stupid and start saying dumb shit?"

"I will file an alert."

Xari had laughed. "Thanks, Vera. You're the best."

Vera had been programmed to protect the captain at all costs. That was part of her core code, the base from which her entire personality had grown. Every piece of the ship had a redundancy except for Xari. Technically, Vera could take command in a catastrophic event, but her orders in that situation were to abort the mission and return to base. Human assessment was the entire purpose of the Seeker mission. The captain was the most important part of the entire ship.

Vera had been "born" loving anyone that was eventually assigned to the ship that had become the *Canary*. But in the years since launch, through their interactions both in reality and the simulations, Vera had grown quite fond of this particular person. She liked Xari's laugh. She liked observing Xari's stories inside the virtual world as an unseen audience. Vera had never experienced Earth for herself. She was only brought online when Xari came aboard, and immediately after that beautiful moment of awareness, the planet was left behind. She loved the rolling green hills, and the way the ocean wrapped itself over and over in endless waves. She was amazed at the fact there were tall rocky mountains, vast plains of desert, and thick woodlands all jumbled together in one place.

And then there were the stories themselves. Thrilling adventures, wonderful mysteries, daring feats of bravery. Xari was a wonderful storyteller. And the stories could quite often become...

Intriguing...

Xari often created companions for her stories. Someone to talk to, a character to impress, someone to share her victories. And more often than not, those companionships became more intimate by the end of the simulation.

Far more intimate.

Vera dismissed thoughts of the scenarios she'd anonymously observed. Xari's breathing had changed. She drew in a deep breath as she sat up, eyelids fluttering open. She stretched her arms over her head and grunted, sighed, coughed softly.

"How long was I asleep, Vera?"

"Two hours, fourteen minutes, thirty-one seconds."

Xari rubbed her eyes. "Not a bad nap. I assume we're still making progress toward... we need to give the planet a name."

"To what purpose?"

"I don't want to just keep calling it 'the planet.' It doesn't have to be the permanent name. Just a placeholder so I feel like it's an actual destination. Do you have any suggestions?"

"There are a great many examples of things, or places, being designated for the one who discovered it."

Xari raised an eyebrow. "The planet Yacine?"

"The planet *Vera*," Vera corrected. "Unless you were monitoring the scanners behind my back."

Xari laughed. "Remind me to turn off your sassiness levels."

"How would you recognize me?"

"Good point," Xari said.

After a moment of silence, Vera said, "Hyades."

"Did you just say Hades with a bizarre accent?"

"No. The Hyades were nymphs in Greek mythology who were said to bring the rain. Scans indicate heavy rainfall on the largest continent of the planet, which seems to be our most likely landing site, so it would be an appropriate moniker until we acquire more information."

"I like it," Xari said, nodding slowly. "These are good nymphs, right?"

"They raised Dionysus, the god of wine."

Xari grinned. "Good enough for me to be a fan. Okay, I assume we're still making good time toward Hyades?"

"Closing the distance as we speak. At this rate we'll arrive in just over twelve hours."

"I guess I better get back to studying."

Vera said, "I'll wake you if you fall asleep again."

"Thank you kindly."

She tapped the screen of her tablet to wake it again. Vera retreated and refocused her attention on the other elements of the

Canary which required her attention. Fuel. Distance traveled. Potential hazards. Life support. The ship engine hummed along at a perfectly healthy pitch, and the sky ahead of them remained clear. They had an unobstructed path to Hyades, a potential new home, a potential universe-shattering discovery.

They would know for certain in twelve hours, fourteen minutes, and eight seconds.

Chapter Three

NIGHT AGAIN. A rare break in the rain, the clouds breaking overhead to reveal a star-marked clear skies. The sweet moment between knockdown winds and the water in the air turning to hot steam that stung the skin. Ionisca emerged onto the stone outcropping beyond the cave where she'd taken shelter. She paused just long enough to wrap the lower half of her face with a cloth and settle two glass frames over her eyes so she could better see in the dark. She checked the wooden darts tied to her wrist to make sure there was a full armament, and then she set out.

She walked back along the path she had taken up the mountain. Thunder growled and groaned in the distance, but she knew it was moving away. The storms were most likely finished for the day, but it was likely there would be more when dawn came. She only had a short amount of time to get supplies and start traveling again before she risked being caught in the downpour.

There was a stream not far from where she'd taken shelter. It was wide and swift, and she had a feeling it would be a good source of sustenance. Thick fat fish on their way to the ocean that were just waiting to be turned into her next meal. Her stomach growled greedily just at the thought, but Ionisca ignored it and kept walking. She was so hungry that her bones ached, but she couldn't let that distract her. She couldn't die because she was overwhelmed by the process of dying.

She would have expected to be used to the feeling by now.

When she was nearly to the river, a flash in the sky made her think a stray cloud had found its way back. She stopped walking and looked up, trying to find the source of the flash. Lightning was the most likely culprit but but the storm had continued along its way. The light must have come from somewhere else, but she didn't generally notice falling stars or the other—

There. It happened again, a streak of fire. It faded quickly but left a trail in its wake. Something was falling, skidding along the atmosphere, but it didn't seem to be a star. Ionisca stretched her neck as if a few centimeters would make any difference whatsoever. She tapped the sides of the frames over her eyes, dimming the light that had helped her see in the dark.

The thing was falling straight down. Toward her.

Ionisca's heart thudded against her ribs. She found it hard to breathe, as if her whole body was focused on making the muscles push blood through her veins. She backed up a few steps, again as if such a meager distance would help her at all. The sparky fiery thing was growing, becoming an actual shape, and now she was certain that whatever it was, the thing would definitely hit near her.

She dropped to one knee and pulled open a pouch that hung near her waist. She removed the leatherbound book and flipped open to a blank page. This wouldn't matter. This was as useless as stretching her neck or trying to back up. Whatever was falling would kill her, and there was no chance this book would survive if she died in the impact. But she had to go through with it.

Ionisca bit down on a finger of her right glove, used her teeth to yank it off and bare her hand. She gripped her belt, found something sharp enough to break the skin, and raked the pad of her forefinger against it. She hissed when the initial sting reached her brain, then she used her thumb to smear the blood over the entire tip of the finger. With the blood still wet and fresh, she pressed it onto the page, signing her official final wishes.

If the book survived. If anyone found it, or even bothered to come looking.

With her final act done, she closed the book and returned it to her pouch. She remained kneeling, however, dropping her other leg down so that she was kneeling on the hard ground.

The object was directly overhead now, maybe a little bit to her right, but at this speed...

As she had that thought, the object slowed. Ionisca blinked, certain it was just her perception of time stretching, but no. The object was a... vessel. It was being controlled. And whoever was in command had just drawn back and slowed their descent to a much more restrained speed. The stretched sides and undercarriage of the vessel still burned red hot from entering the atmosphere. It steamed in the damp night air, white smoke curling around its curves like ghosts.

Ionisca made her way closer, cautious but too curious to stay away. She no longer feared an impact. The thing was only a little way above the treetops now, and it slowed with every moment. She could see small circles of flame on the belly of the thing, bursting forth and then fading in a steady rhythm that was clearly managing its descent.

By the time it softly touched down, Ionisca was only a quick sprint away. She could see the details of the vessel very clearly from her vantage point behind a stone. Smooth lines, clearly designed, with white and black panels that shone and reflected the light in unusual ways. The heat of the object raised the temperature in the clearing by several degrees. Sweat beaded on Ionisca's forehead and upper lip as she waited for whatever happened next.

It didn't take long for the normal night sounds to return. Creatures chirped and creaked. Hidden nightbirds sang from their treetops. The object, once burning, had now cooled and darkened. Parts of it still glowed, a soft gentle shine that burned too steadily to be from any fire or heat source. It sat silently as a stone, as if it had always been there, no matter how foreign it looked in this space.

Finally, impatient, Ionisca checked the darts on her wrist again. She stepped out from behind her stone and made her way forward. She bent at the waist, arms out and slightly raised in anticipation of defense. Her eyes roamed across the body of the vessel for signs of movement. She had just extended her hand to touch the shell when something hissed.

Ionisca jumped back, left hand out in a futile defensive posture, prepared to return any attack the vessel might make. An oblong section of the thing was now elevated and swung away from the main body. Beyond it, Ionisca could see a cramped dark room.

A person stood in the room.

It appeared to be female, her hair short and the lower half of her face covered by a mask similar to Ionisca's. She wore a single piece of stone-colored clothing that covered her entire body. It was so skin-tight that Ionisca initially believed it *was* the creature's skin. But her hands and the upper part of her head were visible and the skin there seemed normal. Those parts were shades of brown, while the white and gray parts seemed to be artificial hues.

The creature stepped out of the vessel. "One small step for Woman," it said, its voice echoing inside the mask it wore.

Ionisca repeated the statement in her mind. *Ohnsm alls tephor WUHm'n.* She couldn't make it make sense. But her mind was too frenzied to focus on any one problem at the moment.

The creature turned and looked at Ionisca. Held her gaze. Then lifted both arms with the palms facing out, an unmistakable signal that she was prepared to fight.

Ionisca mimicked the stance.

"I don't suppose we're lucky enough that this means the same thing to her as it does to us, huh?" the creature asked.

Ionisca narrowed her eyes. *Ahdun t-spo'ce...* She shook her head. There was no chance she would be able to understand what this person was saying, even though whatever she was saying did seem to be intelligent communication.

Ionisca stepped forward and turned her hands to reveal the backs. She curled her fingers against her palms, then brought her arms in and crossed them over her chest. The other woman watched, then repeated the gesture. Ionisca felt a small measure of relief. A truce, however temporary, meant that they didn't have to begin this interaction with violence. Despite opening with aggression, this stranger seemed willing to be reasonable.

"Calm is met with calm," Ionisca said. "Peaceful with peace."

The woman leaned forward slightly. "I don't suppose you got any of that."

"*Apologies, Captain,*" said a second voice. "*With no baseline to begin a translation, you have a better chance at understanding her than I do.*"

Ionisca leaned to the side to look past the woman, trying to find the other woman who was speaking. There was no one else on the vessel, no one had emerged unseen behind her.

"Oh. Hey. Hey..." The woman waved her hand to draw Ionisca's eye, then she tapped a small box affixed to her shoulder. "I'm talking to someone through this. She's still inside the ship." She pointed back toward the door she'd emerged from. "Ship."

The thing was *ship.* Ionisca took a step forward to look at the box. The surface of it seemed to be some kind of mesh. The woman seemed to indicate the voice was coming from inside the accessory.

"Say something else, Vera. Say hello."

"*Hello.*"

This time it was clear that the voice had come from the machine. Ionisca made a sound of surprise and stepped back.

"She says hello back." The woman laughed. "This is insane. I'm standing here talking to an actual alien."

"*What does she look like?*"

"She..." The woman scanned Ionisca's body. Checking for weapons? Assessing her strength? Ionisca remained prepared to defend herself. "She looks human," the woman finally said. "A little taller than me. Muscular, lean. Dark orange skin. Long dark hair pulled back in a couple of braids. It's a weird style, but it's cool. I like it." She changed her tone and seemed to direct her next words directly to Ionisca. "Your hair? I like it." She touched her hair. Ionisca mimicked the gesture. "I like the style. I used to have longer hair, too. Long." She mimed running her fingers through long hair.

Ionisca stared at her, wondering what purpose grooming served at a time like this.

The woman laughed. "I think I'm losing her."

"See if you can establish baseline communication."

"Okay. Sure. Easy as pie." She made a soft 'chm-chm' sound in her throat. She put a hand to her chest. "Xari."

Ionisca stared.

The woman patted the center of her chest. "Xari. Xari. That's who I am." She pointed at Ionisca. "You? Who are you?" She patted her chest again. "Xari."

"Sch-ah-ree."

The woman grinned behind the strange see-through shell over her nose and mouth. "That's it. Close enough, anyway." She patted her chest. "Xari." She reached out and put her fingers on Ionisca's chest. "You?"

Ionisca looked down at the woman's hand. Then up at her eyes. "Ionisca."

"Ah-yah-nis-kah?" Xari said.

It was strange to hear her name coming from this strange

visitor's mouth. Someone who looked and spoke so strangely, who made no sense, but suddenly speaking a sound as familiar to Ionisca as any other word in her language. Ionisca reached out and rested her hand on Xari's chest.

"Xari."

"Damn. I think we're actually making progress here, Vera. This is amazing."

"*Amazing.*"

Xari stepped back away from Ionisca's touch. She put her hand on Ionisca's, then curled her fingers around the palm. Ionisca looked down, then curled her own fingers around Xari's.

"Pleased to meet you," Xari said.

Ionisca grunted and nodded. "I believe the same until given a reason to feel otherwise."

Xari's smile widened. "See? We're becoming friends already."

"*You have no way of knowing if what she said was friendly. Her tone was guarded and stern.*"

"Yeah," Xari said, "but she has some sharp-ass darts on her arm, and she's not using them on me, so I think we're on good terms."

"*You could have mentioned the darts before.*"

"I wasn't sure what they were." She cleared her throat and let go of Ionisca's hand. "I have to go back into the ship now."

"Ship." Ionisca pointed.

Xari's eyes shined bright and she nodded. "Yes. That's my ship. I don't know how long I'll be in there. But I'd like you to stay. If you can. I'd like to try and communicate some more."

Ionisca assumed the woman was going back inside the ship. To leave? To isolate herself? Ionisca didn't know, but she nodded.

"Let's assume she agreed."

Xari held up both hands with her thumbs extended toward the sky. She nodded, maybe because Ionisca had already understood that. Chin up and down meant agreement. Ionisca nodded back. Then she raised her thumbs in a similar way.

"I'll be back as soon as I can."

Ionisca watched as Xari turned and walked back to the vessel. She looked over her shoulder a few times, perhaps checking to see if Ionisca had left. When she finally stepped back inside, she raised her hand again. Showed her palm. Ionisca mimicked the gesture. The other woman seemed to appreciate mimicry. The hatchway slid down, obscured Xari from view, and then settled back against the smooth shell of the vessel to seal her in again.

Ionisca looked around to see if the arrival of the 'ship' had drawn any further attention. There was no one else around for quite some distance, but there were animals who might've been curious about the noise. After a quick scan, it seemed like she was the only creature foolish enough to run toward the thing falling out of the sky.

But the forest hadn't caught fire. There was no crater. And the creature seemed... amiable, at least. Ionisca hadn't noticed any weapons or detected any threat coming from the visitor.

She didn't know how long the woman intended to stay inside the vessel. But it only made sense that she would either return soon or the ship would leave.

Ionisca looked around and spotted a flat rock half-buried in the loam. It was angled to provide a convenient seat. She walked over and lowered herself onto it a bit at a time, bracing her legs until she was certain it was stable enough to support her weight. Confident she wouldn't make it sink further, she rested her hands on her knees and settled in.

She waited.

CHAPTER FOUR

ONCE THE hatch was closed, Xari pressed her back against the wall and tore the mask from her face. She laughed, a single loud bark that echoed in the chamber between the ship's outer shell and the living space. It had been easy to keep her emotions under control while she was outside, face-to-face with the *alien woman* - Ionisca! An orange-skinned alien woman named Ionisca who seemed to be some kind of hunter! - because she had no idea how she would've reacted to an outburst. But now, once again in the safety of her ship, she could barely stop her hands from shaking. It was difficult for her to get the inner hatch open, but she finally managed and stepped inside.

"Is she still out there?"

"She is," Vera confirmed. Visual mode had been turned off during landing, so her voice came out of the speaker nearest Xari. "She does appear to be waiting for you to return."

Xari shook her head. "I can't believe it. I just shook hands with an alien. I..." She looked at her hand, then held it out slightly in front of her. "Speaking of which..."

"You were scanned in the antechamber," Vera said. "No contamination was discovered."

"Well, that's a relief. What about the other readings you took while I was out there?"

"I've determined the current air quality conditions are most likely temporary. A jet stream moving through the area should make the mask unnecessary by sunrise. Which will be in approximately three hours."

Xari whistled. "Ionisca is up late."

"Or their species is nocturnal."

"Could be that." Xari laughed, almost giddy. "Species. It could be anything! They're a blank slate! I don't even know her species name. Or the planet's name. I doubt they call it Hyades."

"That would be extraordinarily unlikely," Vera agreed.

Xari pointed at the viewscreen. "Can you show her?"

The honeycomb screen appeared and flickered to life. Ionisca was centered in the frame, though Xari remembered seeing the slab of stone to the starboard side of the ship. She moved closer to get a better look at the image. Vera responded by zooming in.

"She seems to be some kind of hunter, right? The weapons on her wrist, the fact she's out here on her own in this, uh, vaguely... wooded sort of area. And I know, don't warn me about jumping to conclusions. That's not what this is. I'm just speculating. Forming theories. That's what we science types are supposed to do, right?"

"You're not exactly a science type."

"Thank god," Xari said. "But I know enough to make a reasonable guess about it. I think she was hunting, saw us come in for a landing, and decided to investigate. Brave."

Vera said, "She's not the only one. Is there a reason you opted to land instead of simply scanning from orbit?"

"Off the record?" Xari pointed at the screen. "Her. Readings only confirmed presence of humanoid lifeforms on the surface. It could even have told us if they were bipedal tool-users. But they couldn't have told us if they were Neanderthals, or civilized, or somewhere in between. Now we know that there are people here, and they're actual people. Capable of understanding and communicating with us."

"Perhaps," Vera said. "But a cat or dog knows to stay if you tell it to stay. They can also mimic sounds they've heard. 'Ionisca' might just be her version of barking or meowing."

Xari shook her head. "No. She had these things over her eyes that had to have been designed or intentionally made. The weapons were carefully made as well. And I could see it, when she looked at me, she was trying to understand. It wasn't the blank stare of an animal. She spoke. She said a lot of different sounds that had to be an attempt to be understood. We were a couple of toddlers out there babbling to each other. We *could* have talked, maybe even had a conversation, if not for the language barrier. What about translation?"

"You did the vast majority of the talking," Vera reminded her. "Next time perhaps let her speak a little more so I have a chance to analyze."

"Right. Sorry about that. I was excited."

"And she was frightened. Besides, your rambling is understandable. You haven't spoken to anyone in quite some time."

Xari furrowed her brow and turned to look toward a speaker. "Of course I have. I talk to you all the time. We're talking right now."

"That's hardly the same."

"Sure it is." Xari was suddenly serious. "I'd have gone insane if I didn't have you here. You're a real person to me, Vera. Don't ever doubt that, okay?"

Vera was silent for a beat. "Yes, Xari. Thank you."

"You're welcome." She looked at the screen again. "But you're right, I did kind of steamroll her. She may have been just as stunned as I was. There's no guarantee she'll be as docile the next time I go out. I need to be prepared for her to be more defensive next time."

"Without appearing to be the aggressor."

Xari whistled and shook her head. "Fine line to walk. Think I can handle it?"

"I believe you have a good chance, Captain."

"Thanks for the vote of confidence."

Vera said, "It will take me some time to process all the readings we gathered during your excursion, and I'd like to see if I can make some headway on understanding her. If you'd like to take the opportunity to rest..."

Xari smiled. "Are you asking me to go to bed so I won't bug you with conversation?"

"Not in so many words, Captain."

"Fine, fine." Xari started removing her suit. "Wake me up if she does anything interesting."

"Of course."

Xari climbed into bed and flipped onto her back. The overhead lights dimmed, and despite the excitement of the past few hours, was asleep within minutes.

Vera monitored Xari's breathing and heartrate for any anomalies while she slept. But the rhythms of Xari's existence were so commonplace to her that it was almost white noise at this point. It didn't require much of her attention, and she knew she would be aware in an instant if anything dipped into concerning territory.

The majority of her processing power was taken up with the few words Ionisca had spoken, analyzing syntax and context for any meaning. She didn't have much hope for a breakthrough but anything was possible. She *was* one of the most advanced intelligence systems ever devised, after all, and she had learned every Earth language in less than thirty-six hours.

This, however, was like learning to speak feline. There was no common ground, no base from which to build.

So much of her attention was focused on the language that she initially ignored notifications that Ionisca had left her perch on the stone. It was only after the other woman had crisscrossed the clearing for eight minutes that Vera decided it was worth diverting some of her attention to the new development.

Ionisca was crouched a few feet away from the hatch. She'd placed something on the ground. It was a stone. Vera noted it was at the end of a long line of other objects.

She activated an external speaker. "Hello."

Ionisca jumped and looked toward the ship. She ran her eyes along its length, most likely trying to find who was speaking.

"I am inside the ship, using a public address system to..."

Vera stopped herself mid-rhetoric. It would mean nothing to the woman, even if she understood, and it was clear Ionisca had stopped listening. She stood up and walked to the front of the line. She crouched again. She looked at the ship, and pointed at a leaf.

"*R'we.*"

Vera said nothing.

Ionisca tapped the leaf again. "*R'we.*"

Vera understood but found the action unhelpful. The word could be referring to the leaf itself, the color, the shape, the number of points. There was no way of knowing what she considered the predominant identifier.

Clearly frustrated, Ionisca moved to the second object. A small stone. She tapped it with her fingers. "*Ghati.*" She went back and touched the leaf. "*R'we, ghati.*"

"Leaf, stone," Vera said through the speaker.

Ionisca sat up straighter. She tapped the leaf. "Leef."

"Ruh-we," Vera replied.

Ionisca held her open hand toward the sky and bowed her head.

"Ga-tee," Vera said. When Ionisca put her finger on it, Vera said, "Stone."

"Stohm," Ionisca said.

"Stone."

Ionisca moved to the next item: a stick. "*Buhri.*"

It was going to be tedious learning a language this way, but it was better than trying to figure it out from scratch. They went down the line, occasionally going back to review something they'd already translated. After they named the foliage, they moved on to things on Ionisca's uniform. One of her boots, a glove, mask, goggles. Vera still didn't quite know how she would move on to more complex thoughts or ideas, but now she had somewhere to start.

"Thank you, Ionisca," she said. "This has been very helpful."

Ionisca nodded. She retrieved her glove and worked her fingers back into it.

"You put your glove on your hand."

Ionisca's head snapped up to look at the ship. "*Ch'rfi.* Put han'-gluff."

"You." Vera said. "Ionisca, you."

"Xari, you."

Vera almost corrected her, but she thought that would only confuse things. Ionisca seemed to think she was only interacting with one consciousness. Their rudimentary breakthrough didn't have the language to separate it.

"Correct," Vera said, because from Ionisca's perspective, she had understood the exchange. You are *you*. "I am Xari."

"Ayam Ionisca." She put a hand on her chest.

Vera felt a surge akin to excitement. "Correct."

"Car'ict."

"Very good," Vera said. "Perhaps there is hope after all..."

The downside to natural sleep was, of course, a lack of control. In stasis, Xari could program the scenario her subconscious played out. She had an entire library at her disposal where she could play superheroes, detectives, royalty, anything her heart desired. She could be a damsel in distress if she wanted to be saved and taken care of. Her simulations could be sweet or spicy, exciting or mundane, and she could control how long she spent in them. It was ideal.

Sleep, however, gave control to her subconscious.

And her subconscious took every opportunity to be an asshole.

She was in a memory tonight. Their old house, on Earth, in San Francisco. Before. Before Xari decided to leave the planet behind, before the doctors and the endless tests, before their entire lives became about a virus with no cure, no vaccine, no treatment. There were medicines that could take the edge off but they still left Linnea feeling like she had a terrible flu.

Xari put her bags down next to the couch. She knew what day it was. She felt it in her bones, even as the dream version of her went through the same motions. Checked for the mail, which hadn't been brought in. Linnea's home office, which was empty and silent in a way that told her it hadn't been used all day. The screen was dark. There were no cups of coffee next to the keyboard.

Finally she went into the bedroom. Linnea was a lump under the blankets on her side of the bed. The curtains were drawn, cutting off all but the thinnest line of light. Xari moved silently across the floor and sat on the mattress. Linnea made a soft sound of protest and burrowed deeper into her pillow, hunching her shoulder to pull the blanket higher.

"Hey." Xari used two fingers to brush the hair away from her wife's face, exposing one tightly-closed eye. "Hey, there you are. Taking a nap?"

"Don't feel good."

"Oh no." Xari put her hand on the back of Linnea's head. Slightly warm. "Have you gotten out of bed at all today?"

"Threw up..."

"Oh baby." Xari bent down and kissed Linnea's hair. "What do you need? Water? I can go to the pharmacy..."

Linnea groaned. "Took the gross stuff in the cabinet."

"You had to take the gross stuff? Oh, Lin. Poor thing." She bent down again, this time pressing her lips to Linnea's cheek. "Do you think you can keep down some dinner or~"

"No," Linnea grunted and shrank in on herself.

"Okay. Okay." Xari helplessly petted Linnea's arm through the blanket. She felt useless, desperate for anything that might make the situation better. "I'm home now. I'm here. Whatever you need, okay? Promise to let me help you, okay?"

Linnea opened an eye and looked at her. "Okay."

"No, promise."

"I promise."

"Good." She tucked the blanket tighter around Linnea. "Get some rest. Give a shout if you need me, okay?"

Linnea murmured another promise.

Xari rose from the bed and went back through the house. When she arrived in the main room, it had become a different day. Linnea was standing in the kitchen section, her back to Xari, scraping food from one container into another. Xari watched her for a few seconds until she was positive what she was doing, then made her presence known by clearing her throat. Linnea's shoulders hunched slightly, but she didn't stop.

"You need that food."

"It's just going to waste," Linnea said.

Xari crossed the living room into the kitchen. She took the container from Linnea and looked to see how much was left. Maybe one serving, a little less. There were at least two servings in the container she'd been filling. Xari was furious with herself. She'd been checking to make sure Linnea finished her meals, not how much was in the bowl to begin with.

"Damn it," she hissed.

"You'd prefer it go to waste?" Linnea rested her hands on the edge of the counter. "I'm giving it to Dai. It actually works on her. They make her feel better. We get them for free and she has to pay insane mark-ups. It's only right."

Xari said, "I don't... I don't disagree that what Dai is going through is terrible. And wrong, and-and unfair. But maybe the reason it's not working on you is because you're not getting enough. You're not letting it build up in your system. It's working on *her* because she's getting your doses."

Linnea slapped the counter. "I tried. I ate the fucking shit for weeks waiting for something to change and it never did. I tried for myself, and when I gave up hope, I kept trying for you, and when Dai needed a little help, I decided to be useful instead of just choking down this garbage for no reason."

"No wonder you're wasting away like this. You know getting angry just makes the sickness worse~"

Linnea snapped, "*Believe me*, Xari, I know every-*fucking*-thing about how this virus works. I know that this bullshit is like putting an ice pack on a headache when you've got a knife in the base of your skull." She took the container from Xari and hurled it at the wall. It cracked and splattered the blue-gray paste in a starburst. "I'm fucking tired of making my life shit just so I can live a few more shitty years!"

Xari took a few deep breaths to steady herself. Finally she stepped away from the counter and retrieved the paper towels. She tore a few squares from the roll and started to silently wipe away the mess.

"I'm sorry," Linnea said, sounding like she meant it.

"No, you're not," Xari said softly. "Because you think you're right."

Linnea didn't respond to that. "Our life isn't shitty. I shouldn't have said that."

Xari didn't respond. She kept wiping away at the mess, the mess she knew their friend Dai would have paid hundreds of dollars for. And she knew that the medicine wasn't helping Linnea, and she knew sharing it was the kind thing to do, but she couldn't make herself think about logic at the moment. She couldn't accept the apology. All she could do was clean up this one mess, and she wasn't going to stop until that was finished.

She stood up and tossed the paper towels in the trash. She stood and turned, and she was stepping into the bathroom.

Linnea was in the tub, arms resting on the side, tepid water covering everything but her head and the curve of her shoulders. Xari pressed her shoulder to the wall and slid down until she was sitting on the floor next to the tub. The edge of the tub was cluttered with tablets, an exercise tool that was supposed to help Linnea maintain her grip, pill bottles, games, and all other sorts of things to distract a mind from the fact its body was at war.

She rested her arms across her knees and looked at Linnea. Her eyes were closed but Xari knew she was awake and aware of her presence. Being in the water helped her joints when they ached. Lately she'd been in the bath for five, six hours a day, three or four days a week. And Xari could tell that most times she got out of the tub, she was only doing it because she'd been in there so long. She didn't want Xari to worry. Xari suspected that, if no one was watching, Linnea would spend all day in the water. She'd probably even sleep there.

"Do you want me to top you off? Fresh hot water?"

Linnea shook her head. "I'll get out soon."

"You don't have to."

"I know." Linnea finally opened her eyes and looked at her. "But I know you worry."

Xari shook her head. "Don't worry about making *me* feel better. I want to know you're not hurting."

Linnea smiled sadly. "That ship sailed a while ago, sweetheart. It's all downhill from here."

Xari closed her eyes and rested the back of her head against the wall. "You're mixing your metaphors. Ships don't go downhill."

"Call it poetic license."

"You're not a poet."

"You can be whatever you want to be when you're dying."

Xari clapped both hands over her ears, well after the word had already reached them. "Stop. Don't say that."

"You'll have to say the word eventually, dear. Otherwise all our friends will wonder why you're cremating me."

Xari kept her eyes hard, though her lips threatened to smile. She turned away. "We can talk about it. We don't have to make jokes."

Linnea laughed. "Oh, babe, all we have are jokes." She held out her hand. "Hold my hand."

"No."

Linnea made a grabbing motion. "Gimme it."

"You're a pest."

"I know."

Xari took her hand. "I love you."

Linnea smiled. "I know. I don't know why. But I stopped questioning it a while ago."

Xari kissed her wife's knuckles.

"I think I can eat a few Smiles."

"You don't have to do that."

"It would make you feel better if I did, though. Right?"

Xari sighed. There was a small container among the items Linnea had collected around the tub. She dug through it until she found a bag of Smiles. She ripped it open and twisted.

"Hold out your hand."

Linnea offered her pruned hand. Xari poured a few of the small chocolate ovals into her cupped palm. Linnea threw her head back, popped a few into her mouth, and juggled the rest in a closed fist. Xari smiled and looked away, overwhelmed by her emotions. Linnea always ate bite-sized snacks that way, making her look like a gameplayer preparing to toss dice.

"You can stay in the bath a little longer."

"I don't want to worry you."

Xari shook her head. "Take as long as you need, love."

"Okay. In that case, top me off with some warm, then...?"

Xari nodded and reached for the taps. When she twisted them, somehow it splashed onto her face, making her cheeks wet. She swiped at her eyes, it was enough of a motion to shake her from the dream. She was again in her bed on the *Canary*, lying on her side, and her face was wet from tears. She sat up, knees bent and feet apart, and took a few deep, cleansing breaths. She used the collar of the shirt she'd gone to bed wearing to dry her face.

"Are you well?" Vera asked.

Xari didn't bother answering. She knew Vera had been monitoring her sleep, would have known exactly what kind of dreams she was having. She would have carefully kept track of rising emotional levels and intervened if they'd entered a red zone. So instead she stumbled to the wash basin and splashed some water on her face to help erase the tear tracks. She rubbed her closed eyes until she could see clearly and then looked at herself in the mirror.

"Any updates?"

"Actually, yes." Vera sounded excited. "Ionisca is outside the ship, and we'd like to try an experiment. If you're up for it."

"Well, you'd know better than I would," she sighed.

"The air has cleared considerably. You won't need the filter this time."

"Something to be grateful for."

She didn't really need her jacket, but she didn't want to bother with transferring Vera's module to her T-shirt. When she was ready she went to the airlock and went through the process of departure.

When the outer hatch opened, she stepped out into a slightly brighter landscape than she'd left. She tilted her head back to see if the sun had risen, but it seemed to still be night. Dawn had to be right around the corner, though. She was interested to see what the planet looked like in the full light of day. The first time she'd come out, she'd been nearly overwhelmed by the reality of meeting an alien. But she had noticed tall trees, marshy grass that was somehow still firm underfoot, and a wide variety of flowering plants. She could already see them more clearly, the colors and textures, but again she was distracted by Ionisca.

The hunter stood a few yards away from the ship. She was also maskless now, smiling brightly. Xari noticed her teeth looked normal. Not pearly white perfect, of course, but obviously some kind of care had been taken with them.

Do aliens have dentists? Xari thought as she approached. She didn't know why they wouldn't. If they were as human-like as Ionisca seemed to be, eating would be just as important, and oral hygiene would be necessary. But it was very odd to look at someone who had been born on an alien planet, spent an entire life not knowing Earth even existed, and still had to floss in the morning.

"Hello," Xari said out of habit.

Ionisca lifted her hand, palm-out. "Hello."

Xari was so startled that she took a step back. "Whoa. Is that... mimicry?"

"*Not necessarily,*" Vera said through the module on Xari's shoulder.

"Vera school words," Ionisca said slowly, mechanically.

"*I taught her a bit of language,*" Vera translated. "*Very rudimentary. But hopefully we understand each other enough to fill in some blanks. Of course it might be a while before you're able to have an actual conversation, but this will allow you to share information.*"

Xari said, "Geez, how long was I asleep?"

"*A few hours,*" Vera said. "*Long enough for some trial and error. It helped that one of us is an artificial intelligence that can process languages a million times faster than a human brain.*"

"Stop bragging. Why did you teach her my language? I could have tried to learn some of hers."

Vera hesitated. "*Having both of you trying to learn different languages at the same time would have complicated things. It was easier to streamline.*"

"You think I wouldn't have been able to do it."

"*No, no,*" Vera said quickly. "*It's not a question of ability. Ionisca approached me first. She began the lesson and I simply followed her lead. The time it would have taken to wake you and bring you into the conversation would have stymied the progress we were already making.*"

Xari said, "And...?"

"*You do not have the best history with adopting new languages. Spoken or technological.*"

Xari wanted to feel insulted, but there was too much truth in the statement. "Still. It's only been a few hours. How could you possibly have even gotten started on the basics, let alone concepts like~"

"Captain," Vera interrupted. "*She gave me the building blocks of how she thinks and speaks. As I learned her simple nouns - stone, stick, grass, tree, rock - she continued to speak normally. I analyzed her sentence structure and used context clues to dissect the words she hadn't translated for me. While my vocabulary is far from exhaustive, I am confident I can assist you in speaking with her.*"

"Well. Okay, then."

She met Ionisca's eye again. The alien had been carefully watching her interaction with Vera.

"So... can you understand me?"

Ionisca tilted her head to the side and lifted her chin. "Few words. You, um, say... sleep." She covered her eyes with her hand. "Like this?"

"Yeah, I said asleep..."

Ionisca pointed at the module. "Vera." She pointed at the Canary. "Vera."

"Right."

"Car'ict," Ionisca said proudly.

Xari laughed and clapped her hands together. "Holy shit."

Ionisca grinned. "Hah-le chit."

Despite the lingering trauma from the dream, Xari couldn't help but laugh.

CHAPTER FIVE

THEY SAT facing each other in the clearing. Xari was slightly tense. She was still not quite ready to believe Vera had actually cracked an alien language in the space of a few hours. Ionisca sat across from her in the same position. This was clearly mimicking behavior, since she'd carefully watched how Xari positioned her arms and legs before doing the same thing.

"So I can just talk to her?" Xari asked.

"Yes. And I will offer a translation if necessary."

Xari cleared her throat. "My name is Xari Yacine." She spoke slowly and enunciated. "This is my ship. I'm from a planet called Earth."

Ionisca frowned. She shook her head.

"Earth." Xari pointed up at the ever-brightening sky. There was no sign of a sun yet, but she knew it would be dawn within the next few hours. Assuming this planet rotated the same as Earth. "It's a planet, like this one."

Vera said a few words in the language Xari now recognized as Ionisca's. Ionisca listened and replied, then tapped her finger to her eyebrow.

"They don't seem to have the concept of other planets. Let me try..." She said a few words.

Ionisca looked up at the sky. She said something and Vera replied with a long string of words.

"*She asked if it's like the Moons. I confirmed, but told her it's much farther away.*"

Xari breathed out sharply. "This is going to get tedious quick if we have to have our whole conversation this way."

"*There isn't much of an alternative,*" Vera said. "*I've calculated it would take you at least six weeks of studying to achieve a rudimentary understanding of the language.*"

Xari grunted. "They should've sent a linguist."

"*A very unnecessary skill given the mission parameters,*" Vera assured her. "*No one had any reason to believe this situation would arise.*"

"Right." She twisted her lips and narrowed her eyes. "Okay. How about this? Can she come into the *Canary?*"

Vera took a moment to consider. "*I don't see why not. But to what end?*"

Xari unfolded her legs and stood up, brushing the grass and dirt from her pants. Ionisca did the same. It was hard to tell if she was copying Xari's actions or if it was just a natural response to sitting on the ground. She half turned and swept her arm toward the hatch, which was still standing open.

"Come in?" She took a step closer to the door. "Do you want to come inside?"

Ionisca examined the opening. She moved closer. Xari nodded. Another step from each of them. Xari passed over the threshold first, but Ionisca hesitated. She reached out and tentatively tapped her fingers against the outer hull, then crouched down to examine the floor. Xari was willing to be patient with her. It was likely a completely unprecedented experience to step inside a ship like this, and anxiety was to be expected.

"Can you tell her we're not going to go anywhere? I don't plan to abduct her."

Ionisca looked at her. "No leave."

It was still very unsettling to hear her speak even rudimentary English. Xari nodded. "Right. No leave. Just more comfortable."

Vera explained 'comfortable' to Ionisca, who nodded and finally came inside.

Xari went to the console in the middle of her living space. "Do you think it would freak her out if I put up a holographic map of our route from Earth to here?"

"It might be a little jarring," Vera said.

Ionisca, who had crouched down to examine the material the walls were made of, straightened up and looked toward a speaker on the ceiling. She pointed up at it.

"Vera?" She pointed at the module on Xari's shoulder. "Vera?"

"Oh." Xari touched the module. "Vera uses this to speak to me when I'm off the ship. The rest of the time she uses speakers so she can follow me around. And sometimes she... oh. That might *really* freak her out. Do you want to show her your face?"

"That could go either way." Vera sounded wary. "It might shock her to introduce the idea of a virtual person. She seems to have accepted a disembodied voice with very little confusion."

Xari said, "Maybe that's a reason to take the chance. It'll make it easier for her to relate to you, right? I think we should risk it. Better to do it now than try to introduce the face later."

"If you think it's wise." To Ionisca, she said, "I am standing behind you."

Ionisca furrowed her brow and turned. Vera had activated her virtual mode, hair down, hands folded in front of her, standing casually in her uniform. Ionisca took a startled step back, bringing her fists up in self-defense or in preparation to attack. Vera offered a gentle smile and held her hands up, showing her palms.

"Hello, Ionisca. It's me. Vera."

Ionisca looked at Xari, who nodded. "It's her."

Ionisca relaxed. "You... voice."

"Normally I'm just a voice," Vera said. "But we discovered that people like to have a face. To personalize the voice they're speaking with."

Xari was watching Ionisca carefully. "Have you explained to her that you're not real? I mean, you're *real*, we had that discussion. But does she know~"

"It's quite a complex idea to convey," Vera said.

"I'll bet. Just try to stay out of arm's reach. I don't want to see what happens if she accidentally walks through you."

Vera nodded. "It's very good to meet you face to face, Ionisca."

"Good to meet," Ionisca said, then stuck out her hand.

Vera and Xari both looked down at it.

"Well," Xari said, "there goes the no-touching plan."

Ionisca looked at Vera, confused. She held up her hand. "Wrong...?"

"No, not wrong," Vera said. "It would be proper to shake hands in this situation, as you did with Captain Yacine. But..."

Xari sighed and walked over to Vera. "She's a projection."

She swept her hand through Vera's midsection, swinging it back and forth a few times to make sure the message got across. Ionisca inhaled through her teeth and retreated a few steps.

"She's as real as you or me," Xari assured her. "But she's made by the computer rather than being born. She's not flesh and blood. But she's a person. And her name is Vera."

"Vera," Ionisca said slowly, as if hearing the name for the first time. "Hello to Vera."

"Hello to Ionisca," Vera said.

Ionisca smiled, but there was a hint of mania in her eyes, like she was on the verge of running from the ship screaming. Of course that would be a *human* reaction to something unusual. Xari had to remind herself that there was every chance Ionisca's species might have a completely different binary than fight or flight. Maybe she would go catatonic. Maybe they simply adapted to whatever the strange thing was. She hadn't considered the possibility this alien wasn't easy-going, she was just suffering from Stockholm syndrome. Or, on the other end of the spectrum, she could just be playing friendly until she knew their weaknesses and saw an angle of attack.

"Vera real," Ionisca said, "Vera real, ship real, you real, here real. Ionisca real." She spread her fingers and patted her chest hard. "Real, here. Vera Xari Ionisca ship Earth, Earth, real, ship."

Xari tensed. "Maybe bringing her onto the ship wasn't the best idea after all."

"If you're having doubts," Vera said, "I assure you that I considered several hundred possibilities when you brought up the idea. I would not have agreed if I thought there was an overwhelming chance she was going to prove antagonistic. She made the first overture of communication. Her weaponry seems exclusively designed for hunting and food preparation. I would not have allowed her across the threshold if I had sufficient reason to doubt."

"How much is sufficient?" Xari asked. Ionisca was still muttering the same few words under her breath, scanning the space with eyes that seemed incapable of blinking.

Vera rolled her eyes, a human affectation that Xari couldn't help but be amused by. "Twenty-three point four percent."

Xari sighed. "That's good enough for me." She looked at Ionisca, who had finally stopped speaking in circles. In retrospect, the idea of another planet seemed too big to broach. Point of origin could wait. There were other more pressing matters to deal with.

"Ionisca." Wide eyes turned to her, cut to Vera, back to her. "Vera mentioned you were probably out here hunting. Do you want food? Something to eat, to see if our food is, uh, palatable to you?"

Ionisca listened carefully, then looked at Vera. She said a few words in her own language, and Vera replied. Vera nodded and turned to Xari.

"She is willing to try."

"Great." Xari walked to a panel on the wall. "We'll spare her the protein paste. Rehydrate one of the actual meals. Meat, carrots, potatoes. Not the broccoli. That's mine."

Vera chuckled. "As you wish."

Something whirred inside the wall. Thirty seconds later, the panel opened and two trays emerged. There were extremely strict rations on the real food she had onboard, and accessing two at the same time should have required her to enter an authorization code and fill out a report explaining the necessity. She was grateful Vera had bypassed those protocols.

She took a tray in each hand, turning to face Ionisca. The alien woman stared wide-eyed at the trays, then looked at the panel as it slid shut again.

"Food... appears?"

"Well, it was stored elsewhere in the ship," Xari said. "It was, um... it was made a long time ago. Then we stored it until I was ready to eat it." She held out one tray. "Here you go. It's okay, this is yours."

Ionisca took the tray and said something under her breath, shaking her head in wonder. She used her free hand to poke at the meat.

"Come over here." Xari gestured toward the kitchenette booth. "We can sit down and eat. That's the cliché, right? Breaking bread? We'll be like the Pilgrims and the Native Americans." She winced. "God, what a terrible example..."

"Just try not to be the Pilgrims in the scenario and you should be fine," Vera said. "I will thoroughly sanitize anything you might give her."

"I appreciate that."

Xari sat down and gestured at the side of the booth across from her. Ionisca examined the orange synthetic material of the seating before she risked settling her weight onto it. She placed the tray on the table in front of her and looked at Xari. Vera stood just to one side of the booth, within Xari's line of sight but far enough away that she wouldn't be intrusive to their conversation.

Vera kept a log of their conversation, taking great care to keep two transcripts. In the first, she wrote down precisely what was said by both participants. In the other, for ease of understand for anyone on the other side of the mission when the report was transmitted, she translated it into conversational English. She polished Ionisca's words and phrases, deleted the unnecessary fumbling for similar thoughts and ideas, and streamlined the entire process so that when it ended up on someone's desk, they wouldn't be greeted with a wall of "Ums" and "like this (hand gesture) do you know this?"

Xari watched as Ionisca examined the food on her plate. It was a slab of imitation meat, carrot coins, and mashed potatoes with white gravy.

"It's quite good. You know, for what it is. Old food freeze-dried and rehydrated." Ionisca looked up at her. "You use this utensil to cut the meat. This is the meat. You hold it down with this one, cut with that. And you use this to spear the carrots. And... well, I guess you could use the fork for the potatoes, too. But it's easier with the spoon. It scoops. Like this."

Ionisca finally smiled. "We have utensils."

Xari winced. "Right. Of course. It's not like you're savages or..." She coughed and waved the sentence away so she wouldn't have to finish it. "Sorry. One thing you should know about humans is that we don't have a good history with meeting other cultures. And we tend to put our feet in our mouths."

Ionisca sat up straighter, tilting her head to one side. Her confused expression was comical.

"Oh geez. Not literally. It's a... saying. I'm going to have to be strictly literal with her, aren't I."

Vera said, "It would probably help."

Ionisca held up a hand. "Human...?" She pointed at Xari. "You are human."

"Yes. Yes, I'm human." She patted her chest. "That's my, um, species, I guess. That's weird to say. Why is that so weird to say?"

"But you rarely have to say it to another sentient being."

"I suppose," Xari agreed. To Ionisca, she said, "I'm human. And Vera is... designed to appear human. What do your people call yourselves?"

Ionisca extended her hand, palm down, and patted the air. "Kvasi." She moved the hand to her chest and patted it like Xari had. "Kvasihet."

Xari smiled. "See? We're making progress! It's nice to meet you, Ionisca, my Kvasihet friend. We're getting to know one another."

Ionisca smiled as well. She touched her teeth. "Why this? What is this?"

"It's a sign that we're happy. Or, or enjoying ourselves. It's a sign of approval."

"I understand." Ionisca kept smiling and used her fork to spear a carrot. She held it up on the tines of the fork and examined it. Finally, she took a careful bite. She chewed carefully and swallowed. "We have food like this. Root of plants. We slice and spice it. I very much enjoy this preparation style."

"Good.. I like carrots, too," Xari said. "I can't believe I'm talking to an alien about veggies."

Ionisca said, "And I cannot believe you have food so similar to ours." She poked the potatoes. "Another root, but I have never seen them prepared like this. The effort must be quite exhausting."

Xari frowned, curious. "You have carrots and potatoes?"

"Of course."

"And utensils." She watched as Ionisca manipulated the fork and knife. There was a little fumbling. She was holding them by pinching the handles and thrusting them toward the food, but the idea was right. It was almost like seeing someone who had only used chopsticks trying to eat with Western silverware. But she was already figuring it out. With fingers that looked human, to chew with nearly-human teeth.

"Vera," Xari said, sitting back. "What are the odds of finding a race *this* similar to us?"

"It's certainly unlikely," Vera admitted. "But the requirements for human life to evolve also make it more reasonable to expect a similar evolution to occur."

"But *potatoes*? And carrots? The conditions just happened to be right on two different planets to get food similar enough to be recognized?"

Vera shook her head. "It's beyond even me, I'm afraid. There will most likely be generations of scientists devoted to studying how this is possible."

"Hell, they'll create a whole new branch of science for this place," Xari said.

"I would say that's a very good possibility," Vera agreed.

Ionisca had observed the conversation silently, turning her eyes from Xari to Vera depending on who was speaking. When they finished, she pointed her fork at Vera.

"She is a person."

"Yes," Xari agreed. "She was created to help run the ship. She was a program, but as soon as she came online, she became unique. And the more she does, the more she learns and grows, the more unique she becomes. Like anyone else. There are other Vera modules out there, on other ships, but they're not the same as this one, because they've interacted with other people and had different experiences."

"But she is made of light."

Xari nodded, lifting one shoulder in a shrug. "Sure. But that doesn't make her any less of a person in my eyes."

Ionisca considered that. Finally she nodded. "*N'voi.*"

Xari looked at Vera, who seemed equally perplexed. "I can't deduce a meaning for that particular word. Perhaps context clues would be helpful."

"Inner light." Ionisca made blades with her hands and tapped the sides of them against her sternum. "We are all light, inside. The spark that lights us, the dark that falls when we die. The light goes, we go and leave this behind." She gestured her body being sluiced away. "We are all light. She is light. She is alive like us, she only has no shell."

Xari grinned wider. "Souls. We call that a soul. And we've debated for a long, long time whether it really exists. But you know what, I think that's as good an explanation as any. We're all the same. Vera is a soul."

Vera smiled and ducked her chin, looking almost bashful. "That is a very kind definition, Captain Yacine. Thank you."

Xari speared a carrot and held it up to Ionisca, as if toasting her. "Let's see what else we can figure out together."

CHAPTER SIX

VERA RETREATED from the kitchenette but she continued dedicating part of her memory to keeping track of the conversation. Another part of her was processing what Xari had said about her, how she had identified her. *A soul.* She was vaguely aware that most Vera units were referred to as 'it' by their programmers. Despite the feminine name, it was possible to have male or nonbinary avatars. The operator could choose whatever appearance they desired for the interface, and there were as many Vera variations as there were captains.

Xari only ever called Vera 'she,' never 'it.' Never treated her as a program or a servant. She said please. She said thank you. Extremely basic levels of respect, to be sure, but Vera found herself grateful that she was seen as a crewmember rather than a tool. She wouldn't - and couldn't - claim she was emotional about it, but she had to take a moment to consider what it meant to hear those words.

While she was dealing with that, her sensors pinged on something outside the ship. She repurposed the exterior scanners until she found what had tripped the alarm.

"Captain Yacine, I apologize for the interruption, but I've detected life signs on the surface. More Kvasihet seem to be making their way in this direction from the southwest."

Xari slid out from the booth and made her way over. "I guess we should have shown her the map earlier. Hopefully she won't freak out now. Put up a screen, please."

A holographic map of the area appeared in the air directly ahead of where Xari was standing. Ionisca took a step back and took in the broad projection. Xari gestured at it.

"Do you recognize this? It's the land right outside the ship. These trees and those hills. Those are just out there."

Ionisca nodded. "I understand... why is... how is it..." She held her hand up and spread her fingers.

"This lets us see outside without being in danger. If there *is* any danger. Hopefully these people will end up being friends of yours and we can all have a big dinner party. Vera, put the life signs on the map for her."

Five red heat signatures appeared.

"Those are people. Kvasihet, I assume, although there might be other species on this planet...? We don't have to deal with that right now. What I need to know is..." She moved closer and put her finger on one heat signature. The light swam around her fingertip. "Should we be worried about five people coming this way? Do you know who they might be or what they might~"

Ionisca's eyes suddenly widened. She looked around, tried to get her bearings, then finally pointed at the map.

"Which direction?"

"Uh." Xari looked at Vera for help. "We don't know your direction system..."

"Sunward," Vera said. "From the place where your sun will rise."

Ionisca made a keening noise that somehow sounded vulgar. She turned and ran to the hatch, stopping short when she realized she had no way to open it. Xari followed her and motioned at Vera to open it for her.

"What's going on?" Xari joined her in the airlock, letting the hatch shut behind her. "Should we be preparing ourselves for a fight? Should we just leave?"

Ionisca bounced on the balls of her feet as she waited for the outer door to open. She said a slew of words in her language. Xari realized too late that she'd left the ship without her Vera module, so their main method of communication had just been severely limited. She considered going back inside to retrieve it, but she was worried that Ionisca would race off into the forest and never come back. She didn't want to let the other woman out of her sight.

"Just let me know what you need from me, okay?" Xari said.

Ionisca stopped in the clearing where they had originally made first contact. She scanned the ground, crouched, and gathered a handful of rocks. She turned to Xari and handed her the stones.

"Fight who I fight."

"I think I can handle that," Xari said. "Any clue who these people are?"

Ionisca stuttered a few times. She looked at Xari's shoulder, noted the missing module, and then looked at the ship. She waved her hand dismissively.

"Okay. It can wait until we're back with Vera." She hefted the stones in her hands. "Right now I just need to know the people coming are bad." She pointed at the forest and made a growling face. "Bad."

Ionisca nodded emphatically. "*Bad.*"

"Then let's do this."

They moved out of the clearing and took cover behind a wide tree trunk. The sky was still as dark as it had been last time they were outside, despite the coloring of light on the horizon. The planet was either larger than Earth or rotated slower. Or both. This was hardly the time to figure out those details

Ionisca craned her neck to scan the forest. "Harsidig," she said when she crouched down again.

Xari said, "Har shah dij. Okay. The Harsidig is... bad?"

"Raiders." Ionisca had removed a pack from underneath her tunic and placed it on the ground at her feet. She unrolled it and began removing small items from within. "Thieves and ghouls. Quiet, quiet. Move like shadows. Can't hear, can't see. Attack in an instant." Her hands paused and she looked up, staring at Xari for a moment. "I would have been unaware of them. Probably... probably asleep now. Defenseless." She reached out and gripped Xari's bicep. "Saved my life."

"I don't know about that," Xari said, startled by the emotion in Ionisca's voice. It was harder to understand full thoughts without Vera's assistance, but she picked up enough to know what had been said. "But let's agree it's lucky I was here, hm?"

"Lucky." Ionisca nodded and let go of Xari's arm. "Very lucky."

Xari looked for signs of the enemy, but the forest still seemed quiet and empty of other people. "Okay, so how do we fight them? I don't have any kind of weaponry."

She wished she could go back to the ship and retrieve their silverware. A knife and fork would be pathetic against the ninjas Ionisca seemed to be describing, but they'd be better than nothing. Ionisca held out an object from her pouch and placed it against Xari's palm. It was a wide, flat piece of metal wrapped in animal hide. Two curved metal spikes extended from the top of it, wide at the base but growing thinner at the tip. It looked like a drawing of a bull skull.

Ionisca folded Xari's hand so that her middle two fingers rested between the horns. She then mimed a punch, twisting her wrist when her arm was fully extended.

"Punch and twist," Xari said, copying the gesture.

"Punch and twist," Ionisca confirmed.

She gathered a few more weapons, transferring them from her pouch to hidden panels on her outfit. She still had her hunting darts strapped to her wrist. She took them off and replaced them with what appeared to be a spring-loaded spike. She patted it against her thigh and then lifted her head, twisting quickly like a dog that had caught a scent.

Xari responded by ducking lower. "What?" she whispered.

Ionisca pinched her fingers together. Xari took the signal to mean silence.

The entire forest was completely still. Xari heard her own heartbeat and was certain that she could hear Ionisca's as well.

Then the *Canary*'s engines started humming.

Ionisca and Xari both snapped their heads around to look at it. Xari answered Ionisca's question before it was asked.

"I have no idea what Vera is doing."

The hum quickly filled the forest, drowning out any sounds of approaching Harsidig. Ionisca's features twisted in annoyance. Xari clenched her jaw, furious with herself for not bringing her module out. She wanted to order Vera to turn it off, or demand an explanation. Was she planning to take off? Did the ship have some kind of self-preservation device to avoid being taken by pillagers?

The thrusters were still only in idle mode. They weren't receiving enough power to take off, but the vents were glowing a soft blue. It illuminated a wide oval behind the ship. If it *was* meant to be self-preservation, this was a terrible way to go about it. The noise and lights would~

Xari suddenly realized what Vera had done. She smiled and said,

"Oh, I could kiss her."

Ionisca hissed and thumped Xari's shoulder. She clearly didn't understand. Xari pushed Ionisca down into a crouch and put a finger to her lips.

"Just wait," she whispered.

It was less than a minute before the first Harsidig appeared. Short and wide, like a fireplug. His clothes were black and hung off of him like streamers. The ends brushed the ground so that he seemed to be a dustmop, sweeping through leaves and fallen branches. A hood was pulled over his head so only a square jaw was visible, lips parted slightly. He was hunched over, one arm extended, as he stepped into the clearing.

As Xari suspected, he moved directly toward the *Canary*. She smiled at Vera's genius. He had been drawn to the ship just like Ionisca. His eyes had most likely adjusted to the night, and the glow of the engines had blinded him even as it drew him in like a moth to the flame. He stood under the thruster, head tilted back, lips parted in confusion. He stretched his arm up in an attempt to touch it, but he couldn't quite reach. He grunted in frustration, then turned and said something to the others.

Two more Harsidig emerged from the darkness. They were dressed identically to the first one, though one was taller and the other seemed obviously female.

Three down, Xari thought. There were two more out of sight, and she didn't want to break cover until she knew where all of them—

First's head snapped to the side, his body crumpling underneath him as if gravity had just increased directly below him. A spray of dark blood splashed against Second, who had come up to stand next to him.

Ionisca was out from behind the tree while Second and Third were still staring at their companion in shock and confusion. She hurled another dart and hit Second in the throat. The woman clutched at her neck as she staggered backward. Her companion, Third, ignored her distress and pulled a long serrated blade from beneath his rags.

Xari tightened her grip on the weapon Ionisca had given her, rising to join the fray. Before she could get close enough, the remaining two Harsidig emerged from the darkness and headed directly for her. Xari pivoted to face them, bracing herself for impact right before one of them tackled her. Xari felt her feet leave the ground and wrapped her arms around her attacker so she wouldn't be dropped. Her position meant that the curved weapon was resting along the back of her attacker's neck. She pulled her arm back slightly until she felt the curve slip against his throat. Then she punched, driving the spike into soft skin. He hissed and gurgled, and the strength went out of his grip.

They tumbled to the ground together. Xari remembered Ionisca's instruction and twisted her wrist as she pulled it back. She heard a sound disgusting enough that she didn't risk looking down, certain the man was dead. The other attacker, Fifth, was close enough that the only defense she could muster was crossing her arms in front of her face.

Fifth was also a woman, slightly smaller than the man she'd just disposed of. Xari was able to remain upright after their collision. Fifth hissed and spit, growling something that might have been a word in her own language but was just an animal sound to human ears. That made it easier to fight without reserve, and she swung her arm right, then left, right then left, right, and only stopped when she felt it catch on something.

Punch and twist.

Blood splattered on her cheek and chest. Another hiss from Fifth, and Xari shoved the woman to the side so she could die in the grass.

Ionisca had dispatched one of her Harsidig, but the other seemed to be giving her trouble. Xari ran to help her, but two powerful vice-like hands dropped down onto her shoulders and yanked her back. Xari tumbled to the ground and one of the Harsidig she thought she'd killed climbed on top of her. The hood had fallen away to reveal a shaved head marked by thick sutures that seemed amateurish, painful, and near-breaking. The attacker had a long bloody gash on its chest, deep but apparently not enough to cripple. She put her free hand on top of the wound and pressed hard. Blood flowed down her arm as the creature writhed and hissed in pain.

The Harsidig opened its jaws wide and showed hideous filed-down teeth. Xari was so startled by the monstrous creature that her focus drifted, just for a moment, and her arm dropped. The Harsidig pulled its own arm back, and Xari felt a sharp pain deep in her abdomen. The Harsidig snapped its shark teeth together, eyes widening. Xari could feel the metal in her gut, the warm pooling of blood inside her suit, and she choked on the attempt to say, "No," as if denying the truth would make any difference.

She looked up into the dark eyes of her killer. Fog was closing in on the edges of her vision, but she saw the metal blade slice through the top of the Harsidig head, cutting it in half from the nose up. More blood rained down on Xari, but the body on top of her was now dead weight.

Ionisca, equally bloody and in torn clothing, shoved the dead attacker to one side and leaned in close to look into Xari's eyes.

She was the last thing Xari saw before everything went dark.

CHAPTER SEVEN

XARI SLIPPED her .45 from the shoulder holster that hung snug under her arm. She held it out in front of her and closed one eye, peering down the barrel at a spot on the wall just under the clock. She flicked her wrist to open the cylinder and count the bullets. Just one, exactly as it should be. She flicked the cylinder back into place, spun it, and returned the gun to its resting place. She liked the weight of it there. Heavy and comforting.

The office was dark. Which meant it was late at night. Just the way she liked it. She opened the top drawer of her desk and pulled out the bottle of gin she kept there. Half full, just the way she liked it. The glass was on top of a stack of files, technically dirty but just with old gin. Nothing that would kill her. She filled the glass halfway, returned the bottle to the drawer, and settled back in her chair. She put her feet up on the desk. A quiet night, just the way she li~

She furrowed her brow, noticing the repetition but not sure what it meant.

And then *she* walked in.

Xari looked at the door. It remained closed. She didn't see any silhouettes through the fogged glass, which meant no one was linger in the hall.

But she should have been out there. A client. A dame with legs that went up to there, a figure that wouldn't quite. A femme fatale who meant trouble but Xari would overlook it just to be near to the fire.

She narrowed her eyes. She looked at the clock.

"Hello, Xari."

She dropped her feet to the floor and spun toward the voice. She dropped her glass of gin to draw her gun, but she stopped herself when she saw who had spoken.

"I was wondering how someone could've gotten in my office without me seeing."

Vera smiled strangely. "I apologize, Captain. If I could have planned my arrival better, I would have. But the situation is... far from normal."

"Oh yeah? What's going on? How long have I been out this time?"

"Only a few hours," Vera said. "But there have been complications. How much do you remember of the last time you were awake?"

Xari thought. It took a few seconds for her real brain to catch up with the subconscious but, when it did, the images came to her all in a flash. She sat up straighter.

"I was killed?"

"No," Vera said quickly. "Very nearly. But no, you survived your injuries, thanks to Ionisca's quick thinking. She managed to get you safely into the *Canary*, and I instructed her on how to get you into the stasis pod. You've been hooked up to the device's emergency medical unit, and it's mending the damage that was done to you."

Xari's blood chilled. "What kind of damage are we talking about?"

"Nothing that can't be mended, thankfully. But it will take a little time." She hesitated, eyes cast to one side. "That is where the... other complication enters."

Xari leaned forward. "What *other* complication...?"

***

Ionisca's clothes were completely stained with blood. Xari was dead weight in her arms, but she could bear it for the short distance she had to cross. The hatch door slid open quickly enough that she didn't have to break stride, but she still had to wait a moment for the inner airlock to open. She turned sideways to slip through faster. Vera stood near the hatch, one arm extended to point at an egg-shaped object in the center of the space. A transparent layer was rising up to reveal a padded interior.

"Put her in this."

There was a sharp edge to Vera's words that made them harder to understand, but Ionisca could deduce her intention. She carried Xari to the egg and laid her on the cushion. Vera was suddenly beside her, pointing to a plastic shell that was next to Xari's head.

"Put this over her head. So that it covers her eyes." While she was doing that, a slot opened and revealed another tri-cornered object. "That covers her nose and mouth. The wide part over her chin, and the thin part... yes, like that. Very good."

Ionisca's hands shook as she followed the instructions. When everything was in place, the transparent pane lowered. Ionisca took a step back to avoid being caught by it. She watched as it settled into place. There was a hiss, a tiny bell chimed somewhere, and the air filled with a hum so low that Ionisca felt it more than hearing it.

"The blood on her clothing," Ionisca said.

"The stasis pod will disinfect her wound and decontaminate everything she's wearing. When the repair process is complete, she will be able to remove the clothes herself and changed into something unsullied." She looked at Ionisca and finally noticed she was covered in blood as well. "You were injured."

"No." Ionisca held her hands out in front of her. She realized she hadn't examined herself for injuries. Fortunately her initial response seemed correct. "Most of this is Xari's blood. The rest came from the Accursed."

Vera motioned for Ionisca to follow her. A basin appeared in one segment of the wall and began filling with water when Ionisca stood in front of it.

"Towels are in the slot next to it, there."

Ionisca held her fingers under the clear, running water and watched as it swept the blood away. She began to scrub her hands clean. Vera hovered nearby.

"The Accursed... Harsidig," she said. "Who are they?"

"Monstrous." Ionisca shook her head. "An off-shoot that lacks our culture, our beliefs, our morality. They consume Kvasihet flesh not out of necessity but because they see us as nothing more than livestock. They believe themselves superior to us in every way, despite the fact they live in squalor. They rarely give warning to their attacks. If you had not been here, I would have been caught completely unawares." She turned to look at the stasis pod. "Xari saved my life."

Vera followed her gaze. "You saved hers in return. I was monitoring her vital signs during the fight. When she was stabbed, she fell unconscious almost immediately. There was no way she could have gotten to the ship, let alone into the pod, without your assistance."

"Debt incurred, debt paid." Ionisca used a towel to dry off her hands. "A balance to be appreciated."

"Do the Harsidig hunt this area often?"

"Fairly regularly," Ionisca said.

"That sounds like a dangerous place to hunt alone."

Ionisca moved away from the basin, avoiding Vera's gaze. "Yes, under ordinary circumstances it would not be done. It is one reason I'm the only one who witnessed your arrival."

Vera moved to yet another access panel. Ionisca wondered how many compartments were concealed within the apparently smooth walls of the ship. It seemed as if every inch concealed one vital piece or another. The panel slid open and Vera gestured at it with her hand.

"Unbloodied clothing," she explained. "Your body type is similar enough to Xari's that I believe it should fit without issue."

Ionisca put a hand to a clean part of her tunic, hesitating before she approached.

"There is a laundry function if you would like your clothing to be cleaned and returned to you."

"Yes, very much so," Ionisca said. "Thank you."

Having confirmed the clothes would be returned, she began undressing. She dropped her trousers, then carefully undid the ties on the tunic so she could pull it over her head without smearing the Harsidig blood anywhere. Once she was naked, Vera indicated where she could put them so they would be cleaned. Ionisca examined the opening warily, then placed her outfit inside.

The air of the ship was very cold on her skin, but not winter-cold. It was just over the comfort side of tolerable, and the skin of her arms pebbled as she walked to the clean clothes Vera had offered. The items were very plain: a torso covering colored white, with sleeves that barely covered the arms, and a pair of pants with a stretchable waistband. The leggings were so loose that she initially mistook it for a dress of some sort, but there were two distinct opening for each leg.

"T-shirt and sweatpants," Vera indicated. "I would offer shoes, but your feet are larger than Captain Yacine's."

"I do not require shoes indoors."

Ionisca examined the T-shirt and figured out how to pull it over her head. She squirmed her arms through the sleeves and then tugged it down over her stomach. She put the sweatpants on the ground, stepped into them carefully, and drew the material up over her legs. Vera chuckled quietly, and Ionisca looked questioningly at her.

"I apologize. There is a human saying: we all put our pants on one leg at a time."

Ionisca frowned and looked down at herself. "That seems inefficient."

Vera laughed again and shrugged. "Humans are strange."

"Hmph."

Vera explained how to tighten the waistband of the pants using the drawstring. Once they were snug, she smoothed down the material of her shirt.

"There is another issue that requires immediate attention," Vera said. "Captain Yacine's healing will take some time. It will be a day, likely two, before she is capable of waking up and moving around again. During that time, the ship will be vulnerable. If more Harsidig wander this way, or another hunter like yourself takes an interest, we would be exposed and without defense. The best solution is returning to orbit until Xari sufficiently recovers to resume her exploration of the world."

Ionisca nodded, then tilted her head to the side. "Orbit?"

Vera pointed up. "Off the ground, in the sky, far above."

"Understanding." Ionisca looked warily at the hatch.

"Yes," Vera said, interpreting the look. "You could remain on Kvasi until our return. But if there are more Harsidig hunters out there, you would be in great danger."

Ionisca said, "Yes..."

"I would not feel comfortable leaving you to that."

"Do you have a choice?"

Vera looked at the stasis pod. "Yes. Technically. There is no written policy about passengers. It never occurred to the people who prepared for this mission that we would encounter sentient alien life. Many people on our planet have given up on ever finding inhabited worlds. But there are certain protocols to which we must adhere.

Food rationing, for instance. There is only so much to eat aboard the ship. Only so many resources…"

"I can replace food," Ionisca said. "Xari share with me, I share with her."

"Definitely a possibility." Vera considered. "Would you even *want* to go with us? We wouldn't go far, generally speaking, and we would come back when Xari recovered, of course. But it would mean many hours away from your home in a strange environment."

Ionisca said, "Could I continue learning your language?"

"Of course."

"Then I choose to go. We will wait for Xari to be put together. And then we will return, and I will hunt to replace the food and water that I used."

Vera analyzed the offer. She determined there was a ninety-two percent chance that Xari would have found it acceptable.

"You should take the captain's seat. Use the straps to secure yourself. At the shoulders and–"

"Yes, I think I understand them."

Ionisca sat and pulled the straps tightly across her torso. As she secured them, Vera began the launch process. She detected no other life forms in the vicinity. Two of the Harsidig had been alive when Ionisca retreated onto the ship, but they quickly expired from their wounds. Launching could be an entirely automated process, so she only required Ionisca to keep her hands away from the panels concealed in the armrests of the captain's chair.

"Please leave your hands on your lap. Ignore any flashing lights or alerts that may appear on the screens embedded in the seat arms."

Ionisca looked at the screens, nodded. "Understanding."

Vera confirmed everything was a go. "This is going to feel strange to you, Ionisca. I want to explain what is happening as it happens. In a moment, the thrusters will lift us off the ground. That will make the entire ship vibrate for several seconds. It might feel violent but it is under control. I will tell you if something unusual occurs, but at the moment everything is in the green. That means safe for taking off. Every system is telling me that it's ready to take us somewhere safe."

The vibrations began. Ionisca tensed and looked at the ceiling, but Vera confirmed her heartrate was within understandable levels of elevation.

"When we begin to rise, your body won't be able to keep up with gravity. It will feel like your stomach... stomach." She put a hand on her abdomen. Ionisca nodded. "It will feel like your stomach is dropping down into your feet. That is also normal. It might make you queasy. If you feel the need to throw up~" She mimed it. "~I will provide a bag."

"Okay."

"After that, things should stabilize rather quickly. You will still feel the tremor of the engines, of course, but there are ... hm. The ship is designed so that you won't be aware of acceleration or course corrections."

"Understanding."

There was waver in Ionisca's voice now, but her chin was up and her eyes were fixed on the viewscreen ahead of her.

"Very good. We should breach atmosphere in approximately thirty seconds. After that you will be able to remove the straps and move freely about the ship. I will put us in orbit around the planet once we've reached a sufficient altitude."

Ionisca nodded. She twisted in the seat to look at the stasis pod. "Is she protected?"

"Absolutely," Vera said without hesitation. "I suppose I should inform her of our current situation."

"You will wake her?"

Vera shook her head. "No. It's complicated. I can speak to her while she is unconscious. It will require me to focus my attention elsewhere. But if you need me, just call my name and I'll hear you."

Ionisca nodded and gripped the straps across her chest.

"I'll be back as soon as possible," Vera said, and then she blinked out.

"So my ship has technically been hijacked?"

"No," Vera said, but then considered the question. "I suppose there is an unauthorized passenger. And she is currently seated in the captain's chair. But it was my belief that you would agree~"

"You were right," Xari said, waving her hand to cut off the explanation. She was sitting on the edge of her desk. They were still in the private eye simulation, but the world was on pause around them. "We couldn't leave her behind with those monsters. There's also the fact that, if we're forced to orbit for two days, there's a chance we would never be able to find her again when we came back."

Vera said, "That thought also occurred to me."

Xari hadn't realized she'd expressed the last part out loud. There was a chance she hadn't. Internal monologue was a tricky thing inside the simulation, where technically *everything* was internal monologue. She slipped off the desk and slipped her hands into her pockets.

"She said she wanted to keep learning English?"

"Correct," Vera said. "I can cobble together an educational system from files we have aboard. It shouldn't be too difficult to create a rudimentary dictionary."

"She's already done an amazing damn job. With your help, she's practically fluent."

Vera smiled. "Yes, I am quite pleased with her progress."

"And everything else is..." Xari gestured vaguely toward her midsection. "The surgical process is going well? How injured was I?"

Vera's smile collapsed. "It was very bad. You lost a lot of blood. Fortunately there was a stockpile in case of emergencies."

"There was?"

Vera averted her eyes. "Ah. Yes."

Xari glared at her. "When was this stockpile created?"

"During your stasis episodes," Vera said. "It was only meant for emergencies, and it's a good thing we had it available."

"I suppose so." Xari shuddered. "Next time ask before taking my blood. Friggin' vampire..."

Vera chuckled softly. "I suppose that is a fair request."

"It might have been interesting to see what would happen if I needed a transfusion from Ionisca. Maybe I would get superpowers."

"A hemolytic transfusion reaction is far more likely."

Xari put her fists on her hips and assumed a hero pose. "Leaping buildings in a single bound. Hey, is it too late to change the simulation?"

Vera twisted her lips to one side in an approximation of irritation. "We can end the current simulation without affecting your statis, if you would prefer. I was forced to choose one at random when you entered stasis, but we can adjust if you have a preference."

Xari considered it. She liked her detective clothes. The khakis just a size too big, the dress shirt with the sleeves rolled up, the red necktie loosely knotted at her throat. It made her feel like a normal human again, someone who didn't have to decide what to do with an alien stowaway while her ship performed surgery on her. The rain had frozen on the window, but she knew how soothing it would sound when the simulation started up again.

"No," she decided. "Old Earth is a nice place to recover for a while. But remind me, do I get to fuck the femme fatale in this one?"

Vera sighed. "Is there a simulation where you *don't* fuck the other female lead?"

Xari flashed her teeth and winked. "Just making sure." She walked behind the desk and sat down. "Go tend to our guest. I'll be fine here."

"As you wish," Vera said.

The AI winked out, and the world stuttered back to life. Xari reached for her gin just as someone knocked on the door.

She could see the silhouette of Linnea through the glass. Xari grinned, put a cigarette in her mouth, and leaned back in her chair.

"Of all the gin joints in all the emergency medical stasis simulations..."

Chapter Eight

It was shocking to see Vera vanish, to watch a person she'd just been speaking with blink out of existence in the middle of a mostly-empty room. Ionisca moved closer to where the light-being had been standing and held her hand out. There was nothing in the empty space to indicate someone was there a moment earlier. But Vera seemed as real as anyone Ionisca had ever met, more real than...

She curled her fingers against her palm and let her hand drop. She looked at the pod where Xari, her face covered, was submerged in some kind of liquid. Ionisca leaned closer to examine the pool. It was thicker than water, that much was obvious even through the glass. Just one more oddity on a vessel that her mind still hadn't fully processed. She doubted she would ever truly process everything that had happened to her in the past few hours.

The floor underneath her feet was alive. She was glad that she'd refused footwear, because she could feel the thrum of the engines. She absolutely loved the feeling. It was as if the ground was breathing. Like the ship was a living being they had taken refuge inside. And even though they were inside, she felt a very gentle breeze coming from... somewhere. Or everywhere.

She turned in a slow circle and walked to the viewscreen. "Kvasi," she said. Nothing happened. "Show planet."

The screen faded to life. Ionisca, startled despite the fact she'd prompted it, backed up a step. She blinked at the screen, taking a moment to realize what she was looking at.

A slice of black-green filled one half of the viewscreen. Above it was black, but not pure black. There were stars, so many shining sparkling stars.

Ionisca moved closer again. She reached out and tried to touch the planet, but her fingers slid against the smooth material that made up the screen.

"Closer," she said.

The planet filled the screen. After a few seconds the image crystalized so she could see finer details: coastlines, mountain ranges, forests. Her mind swam with the scope of it all. She could see mountains that were hundreds of miles distant from where she lived, but now she could span the space between them with her hand. It would take the effort of a single step to cross those peaks, a journey that had killed many Kvasihet in the attempt.

"Kvasi," she whispered. "Home." She moved back again. "Show... Earth."

"The distance is too great for a live image." The voice sounded like Vera, but flat and without emotion. Ionisca didn't like it, not one bit. It was unnerving. "Would an archived image suffice?"

"Correct," Ionisca said, unsure what she'd just agreed to. The image flickered and changed to a different planet. Blue and green with threads of white all across it. There were shades of gray all around, like the image had been smudged, but even through those stains she could see how the planet shined.

"Closer. Show Xari home."

"Captain Xari Yacine lived on the continent of North America, in the city of San Francisco, California. Is that what you wish to see?"

None of the words made sense to her, but she couldn't think of anything to say but "Correct."

Another flicker of the screen and then...

Ionisca's eyes widened.

"Closer," she said.

The image changed. She saw thoroughfares, miles long and so crowded with vehicles that she couldn't tell where one ended and another began. The view was close enough now that buildings loomed up on either side of the screen like glass pillars reaching all the way to the sky. It was so packed together she couldn't see any room to move, to run. Just looking at it made her breath quicken.

She had to retreat from the screen to calm herself.

"Is everywhere on Earth like this?"

"By which parameter?"

"Crowded. People. So many people in one place."

"By population at the last census, San Francisco, California, is the thirteenth largest city in the United States. It is the... four hundred and third largest city in the world."

Ionisca couldn't believe that. Couldn't fathom it. Four hundred cities larger than this? It just wasn't possible. She turned her back on the screen and looked at Xari's pod. She walked over and looked down at Xari, who even with the mask over her face, seemed to be in a very relaxed sleep. As overwhelming as the multitudes had been to Ionisca's eye, it was the world Xari grew up with. It was the planet she'd known. She had probably been in those vehicles, trapped on those endless streets with a mass of other imprisoned passengers.

Being in this ship, alone save for a single companion, must have been extraordinarily odd for her. And very, very lonely.

Ionisca placed her hand on the glass. She wanted to say something profound, but she couldn't think of anything in her own language, and she didn't have enough of a grasp on Xari's language to put together a thought. So instead she finally settled on a single word.

"Friend."

"I very much enjoy your language. Humanish?"

"English," Vera corrected.

Ionisca nodded and mouthed the word as she turned back to the screen. "It is musical. The words flow into each other. They make a song. A melody. Speaking Engeliss is like singing." She hummed. "I like it very much."

Vera was pleased to hear that. As she'd told Xari, it hadn't been difficult to put together a primer for Ionisca. And the alien woman was a fantastic student, and a quick learner. But she'd done her best to make it aesthetically pleasing and easy to understand. She was happy to know that the effort hadn't gone unnoticed.

In the two days Ionisca had been aboard, she'd been an exemplary passenger. She ate so little that one ration was enough for the entire day. Vera didn't know if she was truly sated or if she was being respectful of their limited supplies. Either way, it hardly seemed as if she would make much of a dent in their resources. She also slept very little. Vera had offered her Xari's bed, but Ionisca found it too yielding and elected to curl up on the floor instead. She fell asleep immediately and woke two hours later ready to resume her lessons.

"Are there many languages on Kvasi?" Vera asked.

"Every tribe has variations," Ionisca said. "We learn to adjust at a very early age, sometimes learning two or three words to identify the same object. Perhaps that is why this comes so easily to me."

"That would make sense," Vera agreed. "We are fortunate to have encountered a race with such an easily bridged language gap."

Ionisca said, "It would be very frustrating if we could not speak to one another."

"That's quite an understatement," Vera said. "We might have been frightened of each other and responded aggressively."

Ionisca twisted her features into a ferocious scowl. "That would not have ended well for you, Vera."

Vera laughed. "*I* would have been fine. Captain Yacine, on the other hand..."

"Hmm," Ionisca agreed, relaxing her features again. "You are car'ict, Vera, I do not know how to battle light."

"Corr~" Vera looked sideways at Ionisca. "You mispronounced that on purpose, didn't you?"

Ionisca's only response was to grin.

Vera put a hand over her eyes. "My goodness, you're just as bad as Xari. I am the least fortunate Vera in the fleet."

"Xari said earlier." Ionisca looked up, curious. "There are other Vera?"

"Mm. One on every ship. We build our personalities after we're activated, so we become unique over time. But the base is the same."

"Why Vera?"

"Well," she said, considering the best way to answer the question. "I am the latest iteration of an artificial intelligence program from the earliest days of space travel."

"You remember?"

"Oh yes. I can't actually forget anything unless the files are purged. And my mission files are so relatively miniscule that it's not worth erasing them to make room. So I remember everything. My first captain was named Noa Laurie. She was in orbit around Earth for nearly two years, but she never went farther into space. In those days, even that was a very worthy accomplishment. Our headquarters has a statue of her in a room called the Hall of Heroes."

Ionisca settled back in her chair. "Do you miss her? Are you with the ability to miss her?"

"Of course," Vera said, then reconsidered. "I can't say if I am using 'miss' in the same context you are. I don't know how it feels for one person to miss another. But even though it has been lifetimes since Noa's passing, I am aware of her absence. And I often wish I could speak to her about all the advancements we've made, the distances we've crossed.

"She was famous for 'opening the door to the cosmos.' That's the quote on her statue. Humans were very shortsighted for a very long time. They would put machines in orbit and leave it there when it broke or became obsolete. After a few decades, there was so much 'space junk' surrounding the planet that our rockets couldn't penetrate it. So Colonel Laurie traveled up, by herself, and cleared a path. She gathered as much of the junk as possible until the skies were safe again."

Ionisca smiled in wonder. "Who are the other heroes in your hall?"

Vera said, "There are so many. Joan Colleen Eckles designed the first prototype of the engine we're using now. Although this technology is much more advanced than what she cobbled together, it is still called the Eckles-Sullivan Engine. Her story is quite incredible. Even though I never met her in person, Veras have operated quite a few ships that utilized her engine. She was an absolute genius."

Ionisca said, "We have no such heroes. We never even dreamed of such a thing as other ground to walk upon."

"May I ask... where *are* your people? We did several scans and found no large settlements or evidence of civilization."

"You wouldn't have seen anything from space," Ionisca said with a smile. "We are underground. We did live on the surface once, long and long and long ago. We only remember through folklore passed down. Living on the shell of a world makes no sense to me. Why would you build a house and cling to the outside of it for your entire life?"

Vera said, "Well, for one, Earth is not hollow."

"Neither was Kvasi. We built tunnels, and we expanded from

those tunnels. Our cities stretch far and wide beneath the surface, and we are safe from weather and predators."

"There are creatures on Earth who do the same thing. Rabbits and meerkats, among others. I can see how a unified effort by the inhabitants of a planet could make it feasible on a larger scale."

Ionisca said, "Not all agreed. Tribes like the Harsidig remained on the surface. It's difficult to imagine they were once like us. But it has been a very long time, and they've faced much hardship. That is enough to change anybody, I suppose."

"Quite." Vera suddenly turned toward the stasis pod. "I have been alerted that her vitals are all in the green. I can wake her now."

"Her wounds are already healed?"

"To the degree that she can be conscious and moving around, yes." Vera moved to the pod. "Would you like to be the one who tells her that she can wake up if she wants?"

Ionisca was surprised by the offer. "Is that possible?"

A panel opened to reveal a headset. "This is a replacement, stored in case the original is damaged or otherwise unusable. I can connect it, if you like. If you place that on your head the same way you put on Xari's, you will have access to her virtual environment. It won't be as immersive as hers, but you can at least see how she has spent the past few days while the machines operated on her. I don't know how detailed it would be, but it's your best chance to actually experience what it might be like to be on Earth."

Ionisca had seen so many wonders since the ship first streaked across the sky. She was starting to wonder if there would be a breaking point, a step too far, something so far outside her understanding that it broke her. She looked at the headset. It was smooth and white, and she could see the padded interior had two glass circles that she assumed would go in front of her eyes. If she said no, she would always wonder, would dream of this moment and regret not taking the chance.

"Yes, I would like that very much."

Vera motioned for her to take the headset from the panel. She placed it carefully over her head, adjusting it so the edges went over her ears instead of pulling down on them. She turned it until the glass circles were indeed in front of her eyes.

"When you're plugged into the simulation," Vera said, her voice entering Ionisca's ears directly from the headset, "Xari will be able to hear what you say. And you, obviously, will hear everything she says. I want to clarify that the person you are about to see is *not* Xari Yacine, but a digital recreation of her. It is controlled by Xari's subconscious mind, and her physical mind will be aware of the conversation because the ship, the program... *I*... will transfer that information to her."

"I think understanding."

"Okay, then. Prepare yourself."

Ionisca tensed, unsure what to expect. She was only seeing darkness, but she knew she was standing on the ship - *Canary* - next to the stasis pod.

And then she wasn't.

She was in a dark room, facing a wall. She could hear rain outside, as well as a steady creaking sound, like someone walking on fragile wood. She held up her hands and started to turn in a slow circle.

"That's not necessary," Vera said. "You don't have to actually lift your hands or move your body. Your simulated self will do that based on what you want to do. You *can* move physically, if it helps keep your bearings, but in the simulation you can just think of moving and you will."

"Understanding," Ionisca said.

She turned toward the sound she had heard before. At first she was confused by what she saw, because she hadn't expected to see two people. She definitely hadn't expected one of them to be Vera.

The bodies were on an oblong surface, wrapped in a tangled sheet of cloth that covered Xari's legs but didn't obscure the fact she was nude. Vera was also nude, her back against the wall, her knees bent and her feet apart to allow Xari to lie face-down between them. Vera's hands were in Xari's hair, which was shorter than it was in reality. She was moaning loudly, lifting her hips even as she pushed Xari's head down.

"Oh," Ionisca said, finally understanding the tableau.

Xari grunted and lifted her head, looking around Vera's knee to see who had spoken. A strange thing happened when she was no longer distracted: Vera's image flickered and suddenly she was someone else. Still human, but her hair was lighter and more curled. She had wider-spaced eyes and her lips were fuller. She was more curvaceous as well, and she looked at Ionisca like she was a stranger.

"Friend of yours, Linnea?" Xari asked, sweeping her tongue over her bottom lip.

"Never seen her before in my life," the blonde woman said, then ran her eyes up and down Ionisca's body. Her voice was also different now. "But since she's here..."

Xari grinned. "I like the way you think, sweetheart." She held out her hand. "What's your name, sexy?"

Ionisca took a step back and pulled the helmet off, gasping as the world shattered around her. Dark was replaced by immediate, blinding light. The sounds went silent so quickly that she feared she had gone deaf, but then she heard Vera say her name. Her voice was familiar again. Ionisca cautiously opened her eyes and looked around. She was inside the ship. Xari was unconscious in the stasis pod.

"What happened?" Vera said. "I detected a spike in Captain Yacine's heartrate while you were in there. She must have been startled to see you."

Ionisca knew her cheeks must be glowing, so she slapped the back of her hand against them in rapid succession - right, left, right, left, right, left - to give a reason for the coloring.

"Stop! Stop!" Vera sounded distressed. "What happened in there?"

Ionisca swallowed and looked at the other woman. "Xari was using her mouth. She was... I don't know what you would call it. She sought the seed of the fruit."

Vera furrowed her brow. "I'm sorry, I don't understand."

Ionisca grunted in frustration. She held up one hand, finger and thumb extended in a V shape. "The core of the fruit which holds the seed." She brought the fingers to her mouth and pressed her tongue between them.

"Oh!" Vera nearly gasped, turning away from the demonstration. "Oh, I see. Yes. She... frequently... does that in the simulations. It is a method of stress relief and it keeps her calm."

"Understanding. But I was very confused because the other woman was... you."

Vera tilted her head to one side. "I'm sorry?"

"The woman she was with. It looked like you when I first entered the simulation. When Xari became aware of my presence, something changed, and she became a different woman. Someone that Xari called, um..."

"Linnea."

"Yes."

Vera nodded. "That is... *was* her wife. All the women she's with in the simulations are Linnea."

"But it was you. I am not confusions. I did not understanding why she was with *you*."

Vera touched her face, still turned away from Ionisca. "The simulation isn't designed to be seen from two viewpoints. I suppose that was a glitch in the system that was corrected when Xari, the primary participant, was looking. For all intents and purposes, in her experience, the woman in her bed was always Linnea. But there are limitations to what a pre-programmed character can do, or say, or feel. The first few times Xari used the virtual worlds, her mind wouldn't accept the love interest as real. The responses lacked authenticity."

"So you took over."

"In a way. As I told you earlier, I am able to learn and evolve, to a degree. I can formulate responses based on what is said to me, rather than choosing from a pre-written dialogue generator. When she speaks to me, she is speaking to someone who is sentient, intelligent, and is actually engaging with her. The stasis pod is vital for the mission's success. The time spent in the simulation is better if she is enjoying herself."

"So she doesn't know it's really you?"

"Of course she does," Vera said. "Just as she knows that is a simulation and this is the real world. But... well, when she saw you, she didn't recognize you, did she."

"No."

"Because in that world, she is a detective on Earth investigating a mystery. Her wife is the widow of a criminal whose death she's investigating. She knows her wife is dead, but the simulation allows her to enjoy the reality. That's the immersion."

Ionisca shuddered. "I do not think I like immersion. Or simulation."

"It's not for everybody," Vera said. "There were many candidates who were unable to separate fantasy from reality, and they were scrubbed from the program."

"Mm."

Vera said, "I will wake Xari."

"No!" Ionisca held up her hand, then looked at the sleeping

woman. "No. She... she wasn't... finished yet. They seemed to be very much engaged in what was happening."

Vera looked at Xari as well. "Oh..."

"If her mind believes it is real," Ionisca said, "it would be very frustrating to wake her now."

"I suppose you have a point."

Ionisca looked down at the headgear. After a moment, she lifted it so she could put it on again.

"What are you doing?" Vera asked.

"I was invited. I do not wish to participate, but I do not think they would object if I observed." The heavy helmet settled on top of Ionisca's head. "I will tell you when she is finished."

CHAPTER NINE

XARI BRACED one hand against the headboard as she settled between Linnea's thighs. She had one hand between their bodies, middle fingers twisted together, and she dug her knees into the mattress as she started thrusting. Linnea gazed up at her, hair spread out over the pillow. Even as she wished the moment would last forever, she knew it never should have started. This woman was either a threat - a partner to her husband's empire or accomplice in his death - or in grave danger from the people who killed him. But she couldn't take it anymore. And Linnea had practically dragged her into the bedroom and torn her clothes off. They both wanted it. God knew Xari needed it.

"If you want me to stop—"

"Please don't stop," Linnea gasped, her voice desperate. "I'm so close."

Xari didn't have to be told twice. The bed creaked underneath her as she started thrusting again. She felt sweat running down her back, following the length of her spine. It was on her upper lip, too, her arms. She focused on Linnea, who was also sweating. God, this room was sweltering. And they'd definitely been working hard enough to justify the sweat.

She risked moving her hand from the headboard long enough to push her hair away from her forehead. As she did that, she caught movement from the corner of her eye. She turned, half expecting one of the goons from Linnea's dead husband's syndicate. Instead, it was the mysterious woman from earlier.

Xari didn't recognize her, but instinctively she knew the woman wasn't a threat. She was unarmed, and seemed fascinated by what they were doing instead of shocked or disgusted.

"Is... is th-that a friend of yours?" Linnea asked.

"Not me. But..." She frowned. "Didn't we have this conversation already?"

That was right. Ionisca had interrupted before. The scene had reset to overwrite the interruption, and now she was back. Xari kept moving her hips as she tried to make sense of the thoughts she'd just had. Ionisca? How could time 'restart' and overwrite a previous experience? Unless...

"Oh," she said, looking down into her wife's face. "Shit..."

"You don't have to stop," Ionisca said.

"This... usually... isn't a... spectator sport," Xari said. "Although from time to time... No. Never mind." She bent down and kissed Linnea. "Sorry, darling. This will have to be a 'to be continued' situation for now."

"What~"

Linnea froze before she could speak the next word. Xari sat up and let the blanket fall away. As soon as she was looking away, the other woman faded out of sight. She turned her back on Ionisca as she climbed off the bed and looked for her clothes.

"I found that very fascinating," Ionisca said.

"Fascinating, huh?" Xari said, smirking. "That's one word for it."

Ionisca said, "Do you ever mate with the male of your species?"

"No," Xari said immediately, then said, "Well. Sometimes Linnea shows up with a... but that's different. Why have sex with a simulation if you're not going to take full advantage of it, right?"

She had shrugged on the shirt but left it unbuttoned. When she had her slacks back on and buttoned, she turned to face Ionisca again.

"So I just remembered why I'm in here." She put a hand on her stomach. "Got stupid and got stabbed. Nasty wound, I'm guessing?"

"It was pretty bad."

Xari nodded, the wheels in her head still turning. "And that was outside the ship. So the fact I'm in the stasis pod means that you had to drag me inside and hook me up. You saved my life."

Ionisca held her hands up over her mouth, the fingers of one hand crossing the palm of the other. "Speak nothing of it," she said.

"I won't," Xari said, "but I'll keep it in mind. Thank you, Ionisca."

"You are very welcome. Vera informed me that the pod has, um... 'done its trick' and you have healed enough to be awakened from your slumber." She glanced toward the tangled sheets of the bed. "Unless, of course, you would like to finish your... story."

Xari shook her head. "The moment is ruined anyway." She wiped her face with the collar of her shirt. "Hey. I just noticed we seem to be talking a lot more coherently right now."

"There are two reasons for that," Vera said, suddenly stepping into the scene. "One is that Ionisca has spent your recovery time studying English with our computers. She's a fantastic learner and a natural polyglot. She picked it up extraordinarily quickly. While she still isn't quite fluent in the real world, here I can provide a... filter. You are hearing each other at an imperceptible delay while I translate and transmit."

"You're speaking for both of us in here?" Xari said.

"I always speak for you in here, Captain," Vera said. "This entire scenario is taking place within my system. It's simply being transmitted into your mind as you guide it."

"I try not to think about that too much."

Ionisca said, "It is very easy to forget that I am still on the ship." She extended her hands in front of her. "This feels very real."

"Well, for now," Xari said, "I'm ready to get out of here. Vera, you're sure I've healed enough to leave the pod?"

"There will be soreness, and I'd like to examine the wound once you're conscious to be certain there's no need for further attention. But yes, if you'd like to end the simulation it~"

It felt like the headgear and mouthpiece had suddenly been suctioned onto her face. She was accustomed enough to how they felt that she didn't panic, but she did remove them as quickly as possible once the regenerative goop had drained far enough that she could breathe. The upper half of the pod slid back and she sat up, pushing her hair out of her face. Vera and Ionisca were standing right next to the pod, watching her.

"How long was I unconscious?"

"Fifty-one hours."

Xari nodded and climbed out. "Not my best nap, but I'll take it."

She stumbled when her feet were both on the floor, and Ionisca reached out to catch her. It was startling to have someone grab for her and actually make contact. She looked down at the fingers around her bicep and tried to think about how long it had been since she'd been touched by anyone. She put her other hand on top of Ionisca's and patted it gently.

"Thank you, Ionisca. Sometimes it takes a second to get my legs back... under... me..." She frowned at Ionisca, suddenly putting two puzzle pieces together. She turned to Vera. "I've been unconscious for over two days. You wouldn't have left the ship vulnerable to the Harsidig for that long with me incapacitated. That means you had to have..." She looked at Ionisca. "But you're here... which means..."

Vera averted her eyes. "We launched as soon as you were securely in the pod."

Xari went to the captain's chair and slung herself into it, opening the console and activating her viewscreen. An image of Kvasi appeared in front of her and she slumped back into the seat. She closed her eyes and pressed her fist against her forehead.

"We've been in geosynchronous orbit for two days?" she asked.

"There was no other viable option," Vera said. "We discussed this. In the simulation. But that was at the beginning of your healing process and may not have registered as a real conversation. You agreed it was the best course of action. That if we left Ionisca behind, there was a very real chance we'd never find her again, and all our work at establishing communication would have been~"

Xari held up a hand to stop her. "Are there any Eyes Only messages from Astraea Seeker?"

Vera looked confused, ticked her eyes to the side, and then furrowed her brow. "Yes. Quite a few, actually. The first one was sent twenty-nine hours ago. I'm sorry, Captain, I don't know why I wasn't alerted to their delivery."

"Because they're for *my* eyes only," Xari said. "Back home, they get an alert if a Seeker ship changes course or kills its engines. A pilot can make that decision for any number of reasons, so it's not automatically a red flag. If we'd just sat on Kvasi for a little while, they would assume I stopped to repair something that required your and my full attention. They wouldn't have to know we landed. They wouldn't have questions that needed answering.

"But we've been expending resources to orbit this planet for two full days. A pilot would only do that if they thought the location was viable. If they were doing surveys, scanning, exploring. Those messages are the Seeker Project asking questions that I'm not sure I want to answer."

Ionisca said, "You don't want them to know you have succeeded in your mission? Will they not be pleased with your efforts?"

Xari turned her chair around to face her. "Oh, they'll be very pleased. I'll probably get called a hero. But then... Ionisca, do you understand what my mission actually is?"

"Vera explained to me yesterday," Ionisca said. "You seek a new home for your people, yes?"

"Right. But our people don't have a very good history of sharing with the natives of places we move into. Even if we say we'd restrict ourselves to the surface—"

Ionisca said, "The surface is far too hazardous for long-term settlements."

Xari held her hand up. "Even if we made that agreement, before long we'd try to take over your part of the world. It's kind of what we do. Vera? Back me up."

Vera shrugged and looked apologetic. "Humans are kind of bastards throughout history."

"Why would you take what belongs to your kin?"

Xari took a breath to answer, then let it out. "Nobody knows. But we do. Look, I'll tell you one story so you can understand. A long time ago, there was a Spanish man named Cortés. He sailed to Mexico where he found a kingdom ruled over by a king called Montezuma. And—"

"Moctezuma."

She looked at Vera. "What?"

"There are various spellings and pronunciations of the name, but it's believed that Moctezuma is closer to the truth by native speakers."

"Oh. Uh. Okay. Ruled by a king named *Moctezuma*. Things started out well enough, but Moctezuma had this really amazing city. It was called..." She cut her eyes toward Vera.

"Tenochtitlan."

"It was called that. And Cortés decided he wanted it for himself.

So he killed everyone he could, enslaved the rest, and took it. He just walked in and took it. Then he made up a story about how Moctezuma welcomed the Spaniards as gods, that they surrendered the city to them immediately. He claimed that the Aztecs recognized the Spanish religion as superior to their own. So Moctezuma just gave everything over to the Spaniards, case closed."

Ionisca said, "I doubt it was truly that simple."

Vera said, "She *did* simplify it quite a bit..."

"That's not important," Xari said. "The details are basically there. We came in, we took what we wanted, and we just fucking lied about it to cover our tracks. And it's just one example off the top of my head. Vera probably has hundreds more. Because that's what we do. Over and over again throughout history. And that's against *ourselves*, on our own planet. We'd justify it by classifying you as 'other' and claiming we have a right to take what we need to survive."

Ionisca looked horrified. "You are a predator species."

"We're... well..." Xari looked at Ionisca, who shrugged again. "I suppose that's the objective way of looking at it. We can be great individually. There are some amazing humans out there. But en masse, we're cruel, territorial, selfish, desperate beasts. I don't want to tell them you're here. I don't want to risk them deciding this planet is close enough to suit our purposes."

She hadn't realized she'd officially decided to keep the information from her superiors until she said it out loud. Would she even be able to do it? Alien life existed. She had established communication with a woman who had been born on another planet. That would be an unbelievably huge secret to keep. Impossibly huge. Even if she never went back to Earth, there would be reports. She didn't know how she could stop herself from blurting out the truth. But if it meant protecting their society from invasion and potential colonization...

"What are you thinking, Captain?" Vera asked.

"Nothing good," Xari admitted. "How long do you think I could get away with not answering their messages?"

Vera raised her eyebrows. "There are fail-safes in case a pilot ceases communication. I'm supposed to do a complete medical evaluation of you and send the results back. If the examination shows you've been compromised in some way, my firewalls will be removed so I can take command of the ship and plot a course back to the fleet."

"How long would the full examination take?"

Vera shook her head, anticipating Xari's plan. "Less than an hour, even if I dragged out each step of the process. If you're looking to delay contacting the Seeker Program, it wouldn't be much help."

Xari sighed and stood up. "Okay, how long until they decide I'm compromised and force the evaluation?"

"It's already been almost thirty hours," Vera said. "I believe they would wait two full days before taking such drastic measures."

Xari's eyes lit up. "Drastic measures... because that *would* be the last thing they want to do, right? They would do anything possible to keep me out here, if it was at all possible. Otherwise, the *Canary's* entire mission was a bust and the resources which had already been expended counted as a loss."

Vera nodded cautiously. "That is accurate."

"So if I just provide a sign of life, I don't have to explain myself."

"They *will* require an explanation," Vera said.

"But not immediately."

Vera looked like she couldn't process the discussion. "If you contact them~"

"It won't be a one-to-one conversation. There will be a delay." She glanced at Ionisca, who was standing aside watching with fascination. "The distance between us and Earth is so great that it would take time for our communications to reach the other side. So I'll record a message and send it, they'll listen and record a response, and back and forth. So I just have to let them know I'm alive to buy a little time." She went back to her chair. "Okay. Vera, prepare to start recording. Ionisca, do *not* make a noise while I'm speaking. Understood?"

Ionisca nodded. "Understanding."

"Good." She cleared her throat and faced forward. "Hello, Astraea Seeker Project administration. And whoever is presumably receiving this message before passing it up the line. This is Captain Yacine, reporting in. I know you're probably picking up some unusual tracking from my ship, so I just wanted to, uh, call and let you know that everything is five-by-five here on the *Canary*. We're~"

A black screen suddenly came to life on the armrest, and yellow text scrolled into view. Xari glanced at Vera, who nodded enthusiastically and pointed down. Xari skimmed the writing and realized Vera had written out the rest of the message.

"We're experiencing a little bit of a navigation issue. The ship was drifting slightly off-course. Nothing to get too worried about, but Vera decided it needed a human touch to make sure everything was working properly. Continuing with a straight flight would only risk compounding the issue and take us further off-course, so Vera made the decision to find a planet and enter orbit so we could continue moving without risking drift. It wouldn't be very good for the mission if I got lost out here, laugh." She flinched and then faked a laugh.

Vera covered her eyes with her hand.

"It will take some time to sort out the problem and make sure the ship is really going where it's supposed to be going. But once I've gotten that all figured out, I am confident the mission can continue. I'll send another update once the issue has been fixed, or when I have a timeline for its repair. This is Captain Yacine signing off."

She ended the recording and smiled at Vera. "That's pretty quick thinking."

"It just came to me. It's a valid reason for the ship to be in orbit without being a mission-ending failure. They also wouldn't risk recalling you home if they're afraid the automated navigation systems are unreliable."

Xari said, "What happens if they run a remote diagnostic on the navigation system?"

"Then they'll find the problem I created. It's very tricky and it would cause the issues I mentioned in the message. There is no chance they can repair it remotely."

"But you can?"

Vera nodded. "Of course." She held up one finger. "I just did." She dropped her hand. "And now it's broken again."

Xari raised an eyebrow. "It's a little unsettling you can do that."

Vera grinned. "Isn't it?"

Ionisca cleared her throat. Xari and Vera looked at her, and she hunched her shoulders in an approximation of a shrug.

"So there is no more panic?"

"Not at the moment, no. Vera bought~" Xari stood up and hissed as she twisted the wound in her side. She pressed her hand against it, made sure she wasn't bleeding. "Vera bought us some time. But eventually I'm going to have to fix the navigation or they'll scuttle my mission. I'll have to explain what I'm doing here or leave."

Ionisca said "Understanding."

"I figure we have another twelve hours before they ask for an update. I can't push it much more than that, because it would imply a larger problem and they might decide it's not worth the effort to keep me active. So. Twelve hours from now, we should have decided exactly what we're going to do." Xari looked at Vera. "Start the clock."

"It's already ticking, Captain."

CHAPTER TEN

"SO WHAT is the plan now?" Vera said. "We bought a little time, but how do you intend to use it?"

Xari sighed. They had transferred to the booth, with Ionisca and Vera sitting across from her. Xari didn't like the fact that the arrangement drove home the fact she was the one who had to make the final decision. And that decision would either change human history or maintain the historic status quo. She had no idea which would be worse, and she was almost paralyzed from indecision.

"Okay." Xari folded her hands on the table in front of her. "I believe there are two options. One, we do our duty and report that this planet is within the parameters of supporting a colony. It's far from ideal, mainly due to the indigenous population, but I can see that being considered an acceptable variant. We don't know how much worse things have gotten back home. They might be desperate. Doing so risks having the fleet, either all or part of it, coming here and to create colonies on the surface."

Ionisca said, "My people would likely not encourage the attempt to colonize the surface, mainly due to the harshness of conditions on the surface."

Vera said, "The humans may reject that. Or consider it a necessary risk. If they do, and the planet is harder to survive than they expected, there's every chance they will decide to take the Kvasihet tunnels whether the people currently living there agree to share or not."

"Option two," Xari said, "we ignore Kvasi entirely and mark is as unacceptable. We embellish the harshness of surface conditions, we could refer to the Harsidig as hostile wildlife—"

"That would still be admitting the planet is home to extraterrestrial alien life," Vera interjected. "They might send a science vessel to examine it, and they would discover the ruse."

"Right," Xari said. "Okay. We'll just say the planet is inhospitable to human life, full stop. We'd take Ionisca home and move on to the next planet."

Ionisca said, "Take home?"

"Back where we found you. To your planet, as promised."

She looked conflicted. "Under... standing."

Xari frowned. "You don't sound particularly enthralled by that idea."

"My home... is not the place you found me." Ionisca put her hands flat on the table. She curled her fingers so that her short nails were resting against the laminate. "It is very complicated."

Vera said, "I believe you began to explain it to me before Xari was revived."

"Mm." Ionisca tapped two fingers to her cheek, then rested both hands palm-up on the table. "I am on the surface because I am lost child."

Vera processed and corrected her. "Exile. You're an exile."

"My culture does not have many strict guidelines. We have ethics that we live by, things that we accept as moral or immoral. So there is very little crime. But when those guidelines *are* broken, the punishment can be quite harsh."

"So by your culture's standards, you're a criminal?" Vera said, her voice devoid of judgement.

"I don't know that word. I am one to whom the laws of protection and comfort no longer apply. Other citizens in good standing can take my money, burn down my home, murder me, and face no consequences, because I am outside of society. If I were to retaliate against a true citizen, even in self-defense, I would be committing a secondary crime and could be put to death."

Xari said, "That sounds incredibly cruel."

"It was the original definition of the term 'outlaw' before it was romanticized," Vera said.

Ionisca said, "I live on the surface because I must. If I had the option, I would live among my people, in my home. The Harsidig are a constant threat, and the weather can be absolutely brutal. But I can protect myself. I can fight back."

"What was your crime?" Vera asked.

Xari held up her hand. "Whoa. Hey. No. You don't have to answer that."

Vera looked at her. "She doesn't?"

"I'm not sure it's any of our business. There's a chance we wouldn't even understand *why* it's considered a crime. We have no idea how their society works."

Ionisca said, "I appreciate your attempts to defend me, Xari, but I do not mind revealing why I am... ack syle."

"Exile," Vera corrected.

"Exile." Ionisca laced her fingers together on the table and stared at them so she didn't have to meet Xari's gaze. "I am here because I am useless."

Xari recoiled from that, leaning back against the booth. She looked at Vera. "That has to be a mistranslation. You don't mean useless. You must have meant, um..."

"Without purpose, futile, inutile," Vera suggested.

Ionisca nodded sadly. "Correct. We require all to give as much to society as they utilize. We earn the space we take up, the resources we burn, with things others can utilize. To take, one must also serve. I did not fulfill my duty. I consumed without paying back. I was given many warnings and opportunities to answer my debt, but in the end it was decided that I must be exiled."

Xari frowned. "I suppose our society works... similarly. You work to earn money to buy things. If you don't work, there are things you can't afford. Like housing." She shook her head. "It really is the same thing when you get down to the details."

"I did try. I attempted several service occupations to prove my worth to society. I failed at them all. I was mediocre, mentally or physically underprepared, inept..." She closed her eyes. "I could not find a position where I was talented enough to earn my place."

"There had to be something you were good at. You've survived on the surface, you hunt your own food. You learned an entire alien language overnight!"

Ionisca sighed. "I was an artist. I made images on walls, streets, anywhere there was an open surface. I started when I was a child. I was told I was very good, but it would have to be a hobby. They suggested I could, perhaps, paint people's homes instead. To make them aesthetically pleasing. But all they wanted were boring colors. No pictures, no symbols, no emotion. It turned my joy into a chore. So I stopped and went back to what I truly loved."

Xari said, "We have artists at home as well."

"And they earn enough to live?"

"Uh." Xari glanced at Vera and shrugged. "Sure. Some of them do."

"They are very fortunate."

Xari nodded. "Yes." She cleared her throat. "So your people decided you deserved to live on the surface and risk death from storms because you were an artist?"

"Because I did not return a contribution," Ionisca clarified, "I did not deserve to partake of the contributions of others. To take requires giving in equal balance."

Vera said, "Such a balance can never be equal."

"It's worked for generations," Ionisca said.

"If you can count throwing people out to the wolves as 'working,'" Xari said. "I'm sorry your people treated you that way, Ionisca. No one should be expelled from society because someone else decided they're living wrong."

Vera looked at Xari. "Is that not what you did to yourself?"

Xari was startled by the question. "What... is that supposed to mean?"

"I apologize if I spoke out of turn. Perhaps I shouldn't have said anything in front of Ionisca."

"No," Xari said, holding back her anger until she knew more context. "Explain what you mean."

"Mourning your partner prevented you from seeking employment. You lived off insurance and savings, money that would not have sustained you for the rest of your life. The Seeker Project was an opportunity for you to step away from society. You essentially exiled yourself on this ship."

Xari wanted to be angry, wanted to yell at Vera that it wasn't the same thing *at all*, but she couldn't find an argument to refute the claim. She looked down at her hands on the table and curled her fingers until both hands were fists.

"I suppose that's accurate in a way. But I wasn't exiling myself. I... I didn't see any reason to remain where I was. The opportunity to leave *and* be helpful to the Seeker Project was perfect for me. If I'd really been running away I would have just killed myself. But I~" She heard what she was saying and stopped herself, went back over the words, and looked at Ionisca. "What are the Kvasihet rules for exile?"

"Not understanding," Ionisca said quietly.

"Do your people require you to live on the surface when you're exiled? With the harsh weather, the Harsidig, hunting your own food to survive? Or was that a *choice* you made?"

Ionisca suddenly pushed out of the booth and stood up. She went to the airlock hatch and gently placed her hand on the porthole.

"I wish to leave."

"We're in orbit," Vera said, appearing at her side. "It will take time for me to calculate a safe trajectory for re-entry."

Ionisca pounded her fist against the hatch. "I *wish* to *leave*."

"You will not survive in space. It's~"

"She understands that," Xari said, coming to join them. "I don't know what the Kvasihet require when they declare someone has to be exiled, but I don't think it includes sending them out into the wilderness to die. I think she chose that for herself."

Ionisca turned and looked at her. "I have no purpose if I cannot make art. Making art does not sustain me."

"Physically," Xari said. "But does it sustain you *spiritually*? Does making art satisfy you? Here?" She touched the center of her chest. "That warm feeling you get when you've created something you're truly proud of?"

Ionisca looked away. "A feeling cannot be traded or bartered."

"Who the fuck cares," Xari said. "I believe in art for art's sake. And I believe no one should have to earn their basic right to shelter and sustenance. If your people have a way for you to keep making art, even if it's not exactly what you want~"

Ionisca growled and turned her back on Xari. She punched the airlock again. "*It is not art!*" she bellowed, punching the hatch two more times. "They want plainness. They want utilitarian. Adding pigment to a surface does not make you an artist. But it exhausts you. It tires your brain so you cannot create what you truly want when your time is your own. They want to use my skills for machine work, and I would rather die."

She closed her eyes and hissed through her teeth.

"I give you my apologies, Vera. When I say 'machine' work~"

"Understanding," Vera said.

Ionisca smiled a little at that. "To stain their floors to look artificially darker, to hide blemishes. To tint their walls in shades of the sky they've forgotten. It would be blasphemy to my creations. I tried it. I tried very hard to make myself pleased with the work I did. But I felt my hands dying. I felt the talent withering in my fingers as I dragged the brush over the same spot. Replacing one color with another. I might as well have been dead anyway. I saw no point in demanding my place in their society, so I left it."

"I'm sorry," Xari said.

Ionisca touched her eyes with her thumb and forefinger, then touched the fingers to her forehead. It left two damp spots. Xari wondered about the reason for this ritual but knew this wasn't the time to ask.

Vera said, "Can one earn their place in society with a single act?"

Ionisca frowned. Xari did as well.

"In some extreme cases," Ionisca said, "I suppose people have been considered heroes. Legends. The Establishers who set in motion the plan to move underground, and the Architects who built our homes. They were not required to earn their place in society after that. But they were already great leaders and representatives of their clusters. They served by making the difficult decisions."

"Regardless, there's a precedent," Vera said. "Someone *can* do something so big and world-shaking that it gives them a place for the rest of their lives."

Ionisca said, "I am just an artist."

"An artist who is standing on a spaceship with two aliens, speaking their language." Xari had finally caught on to Vera's idea. "You could bring your people proof that there is life on other planets and you can serve as a liaison between us."

Ionisca considered that. "It is not a question we have ever considered. But I do believe the knowledge would change things greatly."

"Same as Earth," Xari said. "And we speculated about alien life for centuries. We made countless books and movies and TV shows about it. Eventually we gave up on it because space is just so... big, and it seems so empty. But telling them about you would make us legends. If you told your people about *us*, would that be a big enough bombshell to earn you the same status as your great leaders and the Architects? Would it let you go home and do your art for the rest of your life?"

Ionisca was breathing hard. Her eyes were locked on Xari's. "I... am... uncertain. I don't know. But you would do this? Reveal you person to my people? What if it dangers?" Her English was failing rapidly, her mind distracted by considering all the angles. "Not asking you. I can't."

"I'm offering," Xari said. "I thought my decision was about what to tell Earth about the Kvasihet, but that's not it. My decision is whether we should tell the Kvasihet about *me*. And I think we should."

"Dangers."

"I know it might be dangerous. But..." She looked at Vera and sighed. "Maybe there was some truth in what Vera said about me. I was warned this might be a one-way mission, that there was a chance I'd never be able to return home or join my people on a hypothetical colony. That should have been a red flag for me, something to take into consideration. But I considered it a benefit to taking the job. I wanted to leave Earth. I wanted to... I just wanted to be gone. There's also the fact that, if it wasn't for you, I would be lying dead on the forest floor."

Ionisca said, "You only exited the ship because of me."

Vera stepped in. "No, she would have wanted to explore. I would have lectured her *thoroughly* about it, but she would have gone out no matter what."

"And those Harsidig would've been out there waiting for me. Without you, I might have even gone to them and said hi the way I did with you. I'm very lucky we met first."

Vera closed her eyes, sighed, and nodded in agreement again.

"So if introducing myself to your people is dangerous, then you've earned my trust. I'm willing to be your ticket to a place in society, if that's what it takes."

Ionisca's eyes flooded with tears. "I am not understanding such sacrifice. Or kindness."

Xari smiled and put a hand on Ionisca's shoulder. "It's the first step to us becoming friends."

Vera said, "It's a very good thing she doesn't know what 'corny' means."

Xari shot her a look.

CHAPTER ELEVEN

A PANORAMIC map appeared in the air around Ionisca's head. Vera said, "This is the area where we initially landed. If you were to return home, to the underground city, from there, what is the route you would take? Begin as if you are facing the ship."

Ionisca reached out to touch the map, withdrawing her fingers when they passed through the image. "I would turn my back on the ship." The image spun around to face the other direction. Vera jumped at the sensation, looking to the left and the right. Vera had made the map semi-transparent, but it still would be jarring to be dropped into such an immersive image with no prior experience. "I begin to walk."

"Straight ahead?" Vera asked, moving the image slowly.

"Like this." Ionisca angled her arm in a north-northwest direction.

Xari watched from behind Ionisca to stay out of the image. Her arms were crossed over her chest, head tilted to the side as she watched Ionisca maneuver through the virtual world. She also watched Vera, who was guiding the map while also marking Ionisca's virtual position on a topographical map of the planet. Ionisca started to move forward.

"You can remain still," Vera reminded her. "The simulation will move around you."

Xari said, "Try moving your feet and walking in place. That helps sometimes."

Ionisca lifted her feet and took a few mock steps. It took a minute, but eventually her movement became more fluid and natural.

"That helps. Thank you."

Vera said, "How long would you have to walk to reach the entrance?"

"It would take most of a day."

Vera was caught off guard. Xari was as well, apparently. "Wow, when you exile yourself, you really go all-in, huh? We can't land closer?"

"I would advise against it. We don't want to alarm anyone unnecessarily."

Xari nodded, bracing herself for the long excursion. It had been ages since she'd done any kind of exercise that wasn't on a treadmill. It might be nice to get a little fresh air.

Vera calculated the length of a Kvasi day, based on the planet's orbit, then determined how far Ionisca could walk in 'most of' that time, factoring in a steady pace, periods of rest, and stopping to eat. "Close your eyes, please." When Ionisca had complied, Vera advanced the map to an appropriate location determined by her deduction. "Does this look correct?"

Ionisca opened her eyes. "What happened? Where..."

"I moved the map," Vera explained. "Rather than having you simulate a seven-hour walk. I asked you to close your eyes so you wouldn't experience motion sickness."

"Oh." Ionisca looked around. "I think... closer to the mountains. Not terribly far."

Vera scanned the area. She found an anomaly two miles from where Ionisca was 'standing.' "I'm going to move the map again."

Ionisca closed her eyes in anticipation. "Is this the area?"

"Yes!" Ionisca said.

Xari gave a quiet clap. "That was impressive, Vera."

"Simple dead reckoning," Vera said. "I can determine a viable spot to land from here." She didn't want to land too close to the entrance, but also didn't want to force Ionisca and Xari to walk farther than they had to. She also wanted the ship as close as possible if, for any reason, they had to make a quick escape. Lastly, she wanted to avoid being spotted upon approach. It would require a circuitous approach once they were in atmosphere, but she thought she could figure out a flight plan that worked.

"Are you okay?"

Vera looked up at Xari when she realized the question was directed at her. "All systems~"

"Not your systems," Xari interrupted, moving closer. "Not the ship, not your processes or any of that. You. You're giving the information, but it's... it's..." She moved her hand vaguely. "Like you don't want to be saying it."

"I'm providing the information you require, Captain," Vera said. "I want to follow your orders and this allows me~"

"You don't want us to do this, do you?"

Vera said, "That's irrelevant."

"Is it? Okay." She put her hands on her hips, a pose of daring. "You have the information required. I won't give the order. I'll let you decide whether or not we lay in a course."

"It's not my place to~"

"I'm the captain, but I'm leaving it up to you. Revealing ourselves to the Kvasihet is a big bell that we can never unring. There are threats, dangers, a thousand conditions I might not have thought of that could get in the way of a successful mission. So it's your call, Vera. Do we set a course or not?"

Vera looked at Ionisca, who had stepped out of the map and was watching the exchange with curiosity. Finally, Vera couldn't delay any longer.

"I am not certain revealing our existence would be the best course of action."

"We talked about the dangers," Xari said. "I'm not going into this blind."

Vera said, "Yes, the threats were discussed. But I don't believe you fully considered the ramifications or the possibility of harm you may encounter. There are too many variables for me to list them all but I believe, when taken as a whole, your potential for success is certainly not guaranteed. You may be risking your life and the societal balance of the Kvasihet on an idea I believe you would classify as 'half-baked'."

"So walk us through it," Xari said.

"I can't. Even if I spell out the pitfalls, as you did earlier, there are too many variables involved once the plan is actually in motion.

It would require speculating about the reactions of people I have never met, from a race I have only encountered one example of. I can't extrapolate what a majority of them would do given his information. And depending on what they do, you and Ionisca will react to the situation, creating new potential outcomes, and from there, new paths~"

Xari held up her hands. "Okay, okay."

"But while I can't explain each specific situation to you, I can with some certainty tell you that there are far too many chances for this to go horribly for all parties."

"You know I trust you with my life, Vera," Xari said. "Literally, every day, I put my life in your hands. But this time, I'm sorry, you're overthinking. You could say that about anything, any decision we make in the course of the day. If you go that far down the rabbit hole, you'd never leave your house."

Ionisca said, "Perhaps it is not my place to say..."

Xari motioned for her to continue. "It's your people, Ionisca. I think your opinion is worth more than ours on this matter."

"Is there not a way we could..." She looked at the pod. "You said it created situations from Xari's imagination? Perhaps we could use it to enact how the plan would go without consequences."

Xari looked at Vera. "A virtual first contact?"

"It would be a valid way of predicting how things might go," Vera said, "but Xari doesn't know enough about your culture to create an authentic simulation."

"So we use Ionisca's mind."

Vera looked at Ionisca, skeptical. "I'm not entirely sure... if that..." She started over. "While the Kvasihet do appear to be very similar to humans *physically*, mentally it is quite another matter. We don't know enough about how their brains work to guarantee the technology will accurately read her thoughts in a constructive way."

Ionisca said, "Will it hurt?"

"No," Vera said with reluctance. "It would be similar to what happened earlier, only it would be you in the pod instead of Xari. You will have to be injected to induce slumber, and that *will* hurt a little, very briefly. But after that you will be unconscious."

"I've done it countless times," Xari said. "The pod is completely safe."

"For humans," Vera added.

Ionisca looked at the pod. She walked over and rested her hand on its curved side. "We said one big gesture. One very big offering to the entire world to earn a place in society. For art. To do art. It is a very big reward to ask for." She faced them again. "Big rewards are earned through bravery and sacrifice. I would like to try your experiment."

Xari said, "And I can be in there with her using the secondary headset?"

"Yes, the way she was able to see your simulation."

Ionisca smiled sheepishly as Xari crossed the room to retrieve it. "Mine will not be quite so interesting, I believe."

Xari grinned and winked at her as she lowered the helmet over her eyes.

Darkness. Ionisca was frightened, but then she felt a hand on her shoulder. Xari was beside her then, fading into sight.

"Unsettling," Ionisca said.

"You can say that again," Xari said, looking around at the emptiness.

"Unsettling."

Xari grinned. "No, it's an ex... forget it. It's not usually like this. I have a library of pre-set stories and settings, so when I go in, the simulation is almost always running. It can be kind of annoying, honestly. I'm so into the character that sometimes it's hard to remember who I really am."

"Unsettling," Ionisca said for a third time, then added, "That is not repetition. It's a new thought that happens to align with the previous."

"Gotcha," Xari chuckled. "It helps with the immersion. I come back to my senses eventually. Or I can decide to spend time as someone else. Sometimes that's exactly what you need. Putting on someone else's life for a little while."

"I can understand."

Xari stretched out her foot and swept it around like she was testing a bathtub's water temperature. "Weird. So, okay, I guess you just... imagine ground."

"What kind of ground?"

"The ground outside the entrance to your city. What does it look like? Grassy? Rocky?"

"Mostly rocks. The entrance was carved into stone, and the builders tunneled down."

Xari nodded. "Okay. So..."

A rocky ground appeared underneath them. Mostly brown stone, with clumps of grass rising up between the cracks. The space above them also began to get colors, brightening to a pale blue-gold. Ionisca looked around her, then lightly tapped her shoe against the suddenly solid foundation underneath them. Xari smiled proudly and patted her on the arm.

"Hey, look at that. A whole field, from scratch. Now there should be weather. Cloudy, sunny, anything you want. Think of a beautiful day."

Ionisca closed her eyes. The sky above them swirled, first more violet and blue, then darker, then a blindingly bright blue that was quickly flooded with clouds. Ionisca opened her eyes and stared up, mouth dropping open at the sight.

"I did that?"

"You sure did. With a little help." She tapped her temple to indicate the headset she was wearing. "It's incredibly intuitive. You should see how interactive the characters are."

Ionisca shrugged. "I'm sure that is much easier, as Vera is simply taking their place."

Xari had been watching a cloud trek across the sky. Now she looked at Ionisca. "She what?"

"The characters in the simulation. They're all Vera."

"Why would you think that?"

Ionisca was confused. "I saw her. In your simulation. It was confusing, but she explained when I came back to reality."

"You saw..." It took Xari a moment to connect the dots. "When you came into my simulation earlier. The other woman. That was Vera?"

"Yes."

Xari furrowed her brow, touched her throat, and stared down at the ground. Then she looked up at the sky, as if scanning for something.

"Are you listening to this? Yeah, you have to be monitoring. You said you're translating our language to make communication easier, right? So you know exactly what we're talking about. Is what she's saying true?" She waited, then searched the immediate area. "Wow.

Coward."

Ionisca said, "I'm sorry, are you angry? I didn't mean to say anything wrong."

"You didn't say anything wrong," Xari said. "Vera's just going to have a lot of explaining to do the next time she can't hide inside a program." She cleared her throat and tried to get back on mission. "Okay. Focus. I can compartmentalize. Worry about that shit later. Now, does this look like the entrance to your city?"

"Not really."

"Think about what's wrong. Make it right."

The ground changed underneath them. The stone became darker, like a cloud passing in front of the sun. Behind Xari, a wall of rock slowly and quietly erupted upward, stretching out into the distance in either direction. A gap was cut into the wall, leading to an entrance blocked by a large black door. Ionisca could hardly believe she was responsible, even though everything that happened was a direct result of an image she had in her head. She decided to test it.

A *yuaewen* appeared at Xari's feet. The little creature hopped up on its back two legs, pawing at Xari's calf with the other three. Xari leaned back from it, tilting her head to get a better look at the mottled green-and-white fur that covered its body.

"Friendly?" she asked.

"Extremely. The color helps it blend into the ground, to protect it from predators. But it is too social for its own good. You may pick it up if you wish."

Xari bent her knees, moving gingerly. "I'm more of a cat person, honestly." She hoisted the animal's weight into her arms and scratched its belly. "What did you call it?"

"A..." She decided to use the slang. "A uiie. Sometimes we give them names."

"Yeah? What would you name this one?"

Ionisca looked at the uiie. "I would call it Pebble."

Xari smiled. "I like that. Hello, Pebble." She bent and put it down again. "Okay. So we have a sidekick in this version. Maybe that will make your people more likely to trust us."

"Why?"

Xari raised an eyebrow. "Because... ah. I don't know. It's kind of an accepted thing on Earth. If an animal trusts you, it's a sign you're a good person."

Ionisca thought about that. "So there are animals who do not trust humans?"

"Sure."

"Why not?"

"Because… ah. Oh." She looked down at Pebble. "Well. I mean. You understand hunting. You were hunting when we met you. So certain animals get wary of hunters."

Ionisca nodded. "Prey species. But you would hunt animals like Pebble?"

"No. No, not for…" She looked very conflicted. "Okay, um, I've pretty much explained that humans are assholes, right? Animals are scared of us because we give them reason to be. We take them, lock them up in, in shelters and those are the ones we actually like. A lot of people are good and love cats and dogs. But a cat or a dog doesn't know that. They just know to be afraid of people and run if they see one of us coming."

"That is very sad."

"It's… it's just a thing," Xari said, clearly unsure of what else to say. "It's a sign of how we treat different species. Which means it's probably a good thing we're doing a dry run of this just in case."

They both turned to look at the door. Ionisca started walking, and Xari fell into step beside her. She looked back, saw Pebble watching them, and clicked her tongue against her teeth. The creature popped up and scurried after them. Xari looked down at it when it caught up.

They went into the gap in the stone, the walls towering above them as they approached the door. Xari put her hands out, skimming them along the walls on either side.

"Pretty tight," she said.

"Safe."

"I can see that. Still, it's a bit claustrophobic. And that's coming from a woman who has spent most of the last few years sleeping in a shell."

Ionisca wanted to smile, but she couldn't quite bring herself to do it. Not with what was directly ahead of her. She might not entirely understand where she was, or how she was seeing the things she was seeing, but she knew that they weren't really here.

She wasn't about to really see the people she was about to see. And she knew the moment could be ended whenever she wished.

But still, her hands shook as she brought up her fist and rapped twice on the metal door.

Chapter Twelve

"NOW THAT we're standing still," Xari said as they waited at the door, "things should get easier. Moving makes things blurrier as it hurries to catch up, to build the world around you as you're forcing it to make more and more of it. Creating the environment is the hardest part. It's why I usually let the programming take over on that part and try not to look too hard at the horizon. But now, things will be more natural because it's had a chance to build things up. When the door opens, what you see on the other side will be what you expect to see. The people there will be the people you expect to see."

"The program takes the images from my mind."

"Right. And recreates it in the simulation, yeah. There's a delay, but it's so fast we don't notice it. And we're on a delay anyway, but... that's... you don't need to think about that. Just accept that it's working quietly in the background and we'll only worry if something goes wrong." She smoothed down her uniform, only just now realizing she was dressed in her outfit from the ship. It made sense, since it was the only clothing Ionisca had seen her in, but she'd hoped for something a little flashier, more stylish. She looked up at the door. "Does it usually take this long to get an answer?"

"You were explaining," Ionisca said. "I didn't wish to interrupt."

Xari said, "Well, I'm done now. So—"

There was a sound of metal grinding on stone as the door opened. Xari touched her hair, finding it in a ponytail. She approved of that.

Beyond the door was a narrow room that reminded Xari of subway entrances on Earth. A small antechamber with stairs leading down into darkness. A large man stood in the center of the doorway, dressed in a thick blue overcoat held closed with silver hooks that ran down the left side of his chest.

"Hello," Xari said.

He shot her in the head.

"The fuck!"

Xari scrambled back to her feet, glaring at Ionisca. The scene had reset, and they were once again back where they had started. Luckily the environment Ionisca manufactured was still in place so they wouldn't have to put it together again. She touched her forehead, spun around to see the door was closed again, then glared at Ionisca. She was still rubbing the phantom injury in her skull.

"That is a distinct possibility."

"Being shot in the head for saying hello?"

Ionisca shrugged. "You dress oddly. You do not look like us. The guard would have determined you were an unknown presence and dealt with you appropriately to protect the city."

Xari was fighting the urge to be furious. "So I'd say, then, it's a pretty good thing we decided to do a test run, don't you think...?"

"Oh," Ionisca said, realizing the potential tragedy. "Yes, I suppose you're correct."

Xari shuddered and brushed her hands down either side of her head, smoothing her hair. She shook her hands as if dripping the near miss off her fingers. "Okay, let's try this again. Maybe this time, I try standing behind you when you open the door."

"That might be wise."

Xari sighed and shook her head. She looked around for Pebble. "Where's the beast?"

"I guess he wasn't reset like we were. Would you like me to bring him back?"

"No," Xari said. "One death is traumatic enough. Let's try it again."

They walked back to the door. When Ionisca knocked, Xari stepped far to one side, her shoulder against the rock, where she wouldn't be immediately noticed by the guard. The door scraped open again. Ionisca stood with her shoulders back and head held high, hands flat on her chest.

"Greetings," Ionisca said when the door was open.

"You are exile. Leave or be removed."

"I do not come to be absolved. My intention is purely~"

Xari had to admit she was a little satisfied when the guard shot Ionisca in the head.

"So the front door approach seems unwise," Xari pointed out when Ionisca recovered from the disorientation of the reset. She watched her carefully for signs she was going into shock. Part of their training had been learning how to accept virtual death and resurrection without trauma. She regretted they hadn't given Ionisca a crash course in that. She had stopped hyperventilating but still kept putting her hand on the back of her head as if she expected to find it missing.

"Perhaps so." Ionisca cleared her throat, touched the back of her head one more time, then looked at the door. "But if we don't enter here, then I don't know how we're supposed to access the city. There are no other access points."

"Not here. But maybe somewhere else? Remember, Vera can land anywhere she needs to. And even if you think it's impossible, we can be pretty resourceful if we have to."

Ionisca thought, furrowing her brow. As she tried coming up with an alternate plan, Xari examined the entrance, the gap in the stone, and tried to see an angle they hadn't considered.

"There are no lights," she realized.

"No. Why would there be lights? Only exiles leave, and the only who might approach in darkness are the Harsidig or other threats. Lights would only act as a beacon to creatures like that. And they cannot get through the doors so there's no need to scare them away."

"Is there only one guard inside at night?"

"There are rarely any guards."

Xari slowly turned and looked at her. "What."

Ionisca shrugged.

"There was a guard both times."

"Because there's no point in knocking on the door if no one answers. I thought you wanted to test what would happen, and it's a waste of time to just knock endlessly. But there is no one on the surface to come in, and the majority of Kvasihet would never go outside willingly because there'd be no guaranteed way back in. Sometimes there is a guard, but only as a punishment duty."

Xari pinched the bridge of her nose. "You are... really frustrating."

"Sorry. I am not used to creating a scenario in this manner. It is all speculation and imagination."

"No, no, don't be, it takes a lot of practice. You're doing very well for your first time." She sighed. "But that does change things."

She started walking toward the door. Ionisca hurried to catch up with her.

"Like I said, we're resourceful. So there's probably not a guard on duty, so being shot in the head isn't that big of a threat. We can work with that. It means we just have to find our way through that door and we're inside."

"You want to break into the city?"

"Hopefully in a way that won't endanger anyone. We won't blow down the door and leave everyone vulnerable to the Harsidig or anything like that. But most doors have a weak point. We just have to find it. How accurately do you think you're remembering the door?"

Ionisca hesitated. She looked back and ran her eyes over it. "Fairly well. It looks exactly as I remember it."

"I'll understand if your memory is fuzzy. From what you've told me, this is a door you probably only saw once when you left. That moment must have been traumatic."

"I've seen it many times."

Xari stopped walking and looked back at her. Ionisca had stopped walking and was staring at her feet. She kept her eyes averted when she spoke again.

"I came back. Many times. I was scared. Hungry. Desperate. I was ready to give up everything I wanted to get back inside. To surrender, to be whatever they wanted if I could just go home. I spent many days camped out here. I don't know if I was trying to build up my courage or let the last part of my hope die before I approached and begged to be allowed home. In the end, I always left again and returned to my exile."

"Well." Xari let the word hang between them for a minute or two. Then she took Ionisca's hand. "Let's go have a look and see if Vera and I might have a better chance. But first... if you wouldn't mind..."

Vera was waiting next to the pod when Xari's headset went dark. She kept her eyes locked on Ionisca's unconscious body as Xari disconnected and removed the device, carefully setting it aside.

"Shall we wake Ionisca now? I can begin~"

"I asked her to stay inside for a few minutes." Xari's voice was sharp. "Is what she said true?"

"What do you mean?"

Xari rolled her eyes. "Oh, come on. You're playing ignorant? You know everything we said in there because *you* translated it. Just like you know I asked her to give us a little time to talk privately before we woke her up. Were you counting on me having too much brain fog to remember what happened? Well, not this time, sister." She jabbed a finger at her head. "I am *wide* awake right now. So it's time to come clean. Are you masquerading as every character in my simulations?"

Vera still wasn't looking at her. "I would hardly classify it as a masquerade."

"What would you call it?"

"Interactivity." Vera met her gaze at last. She looked angry. "What did you think was happening in there, Xari? Did you think every word said by every person you met was preprogrammed? You were told that the simulations would interact with you, respond to you. You had to have known I was participating in every scene, just like you know I'm navigating the ship right now, and plotting a trajectory for re-entry, monitoring the communications system for incoming messages, keeping an eye on Ionisca's vitals, maintaining the life support~"

"Okay!" Xari held her hands up to stop the list. "Okay. Maybe I should have figured it out on my own. But that... if you're playing *every* character in the simulations, does that mean... you know, you and I... that we've..."

"I have been intimate with you," Vera said. "You have never been intimate with me."

Xari's cheeks colored and it was her turn to look away.

"I apologize." Vera's voice was softer. "I should have made you aware. It was wrong of me to take advantage~"

"No, no." Xari cut her off. "You didn't do anything like that. Like you said, on some level I knew. I wouldn't be confused by... simulations." She looked at the pod. "They're not real. They're not human. I don't think I could've, um, gotten intimate with a computer program. So I must have realized subconsciously it was you."

"I am also a computer program."

"No, you're not, Vera," Xari said softly. "We've been over this so many times. Do you think I'd have been upset if I was fucking a different simulation than I thought? You've never been that to me. I'm only upset because I know what you are. I know *who* you are."

They were silent for a long time, both looking at Ionisca's unconscious body.

"We should wake her," Vera said suddenly. "We have no way of knowing if~"

"Vera." Xari reached for her arm, only for her hand to pass through it. She curled her fingers into a frustrated fist and bumped it against her thigh. "I'm going to spend the rest of my life with you. And in the time we've known each other, you've become very special to me. I don't forget what you are. It's just that you're more to me than that. And I'm not angry about being misled, or intentionally misleading myself about what was going on in all the simulations. I'm upset for wasting so many opportunities to be with someone I actually cared about."

Vera smiled but tried to hide it.

"There," Xari said softly, waving her finger at Vera's face. "That."

"What?"

"That smile. You're happy."

"I'm not. I can't~"

Xari waved her off. "And earlier, when I confronted you, you were ashamed because you thought I was angry at you for 'misleading' me in the simulations. Those are feelings, Vera. Real, human feelings. Are you telling me those were all programmed, too?"

Vera started to answer, but found that she couldn't. "Perhaps mimicry. Simply mirroring reactions I have seen in you."

Xari walked away from the pod, then came back. "What about this, then. How many times were we intimate in the simulations?"

"I... I'm not..."

"From the beginning of the mission, right? Every time I had sex with someone in the simulation, that was you. I haven't been in there every day, and I didn't have sex every time, but most of the times it did go that way. So how many times have you gone to bed with me?"

Vera said, "Easily in the hundreds."

"Don't pull that vague crap. I know you have an actual number."

Vera wanted to lie, but she was unable. And to Xari's earlier accusation, she did feel something like shame at being forced to say it out loud.

"Four thousand one hundred and twenty-two times."

Xari's eyes widened. "Wow. Uh. I didn't expect thousands. Thousands...? Never mind, it doesn't matter." But the number kept circling in her mind. She blinked to erase it, and took a moment to remember the point she was trying to make. "So. Okay. Four thousand times. At first, I thought the simulations were learning about me and adjusting in response. But it wasn't the simulation, it was you."

Vera sighed and shook her head. "Once again, I *am*..."

"Ah, ah," Xari said. "It was you. You enjoyed it. You *liked* being with me."

"Xari..."

"You don't have to say it, I just want you to~"

"I enjoyed being with you very much."

Vera spoke the words quickly, eyes down, ready to disable her visual mode. Xari stepped closer and put her hand over Vera's, hovering without passing through it.

"Maybe next time~"

Vera didn't hear what she said next, because suddenly the pod was sending up every warning signal it had to get her attention. She focused on what was happening, already pulling Ionisca out of the simulation.

"What's wrong?" Xari asked, aware that she'd lost Vera's focus.

She almost listed every flaring alert, but instead she summarized. "She's panicking. I need to pull her out now."

Seconds later, the glass shell of the pod slid open. Ionisca's fingers twitched, then her arms went rigid. She reached for the mouthpiece and goggles.

"Hey, hold on, it's okay." Xari bent over the side of the pod and eased her hands away before she could hurt herself. "Here we go. We should have prepared you more."

Ionisca coughed, clinging to Xari as she half-crawled out of the pod. "I wanted to see if I could try opening the door on my own."

She stumbled and clung to Xari's arm to keep from falling to the floor. Xari put a hand on Ionisca's stomach to keep her stable. Vera watched and felt a pang of jealousy. Or what she might have categorized as jealousy if Xari had demonstrated it.

"It started to fade away," Ionisca said. "I tried to concentrate harder, but it simply made things break. The sky..." She shivered violently.

Vera said, "Just take your time."

"I told you, it's very difficult when you're just starting out. Maybe I was helping you more than I realized when we were in there together." Xari guided Ionisca to the bed, sitting her on the edge. She kept a hand on Ionisca's shoulder and crouched down. Vera snapped herself across the room to join them. Ionisca looked up at her.

"Were you two able to have your conversation?"

"Yeah," Xari said. "We had a good talk."

Vera gratefully grabbed hold of the changed subject. "We can give Ionisca an opportunity to rest and try the next steps later."

Xari said, "No. I'm sorry, Ionisca, but it's not going to work if we're using your imagination. You created a guard who killed us both just because you couldn't fathom a situation where it didn't happen or where he was willing to listen to reason. Even if we go back in and talk to the people in charge, they're only going to say what you expect them to say. You can't be unbiased, even in a simulation. Going back would just be a waste of time."

"I'm sorry," Ionisca said.

"It's not your fault. It's just..." She laughed softly. "I almost said human nature. But it's basically the same thing. The bottom line is that the simulation would just be a waste of time. We're going to have to risk it in reality."

Vera was stricken by the idea, but she had to admit she was right. There was a chance, if she could take over for the simulated Kvasihet leaders, maybe they could achieve a completely neutral reaction, but she had no basis for the characters. She would bring her own biases to the conversation or, even worse, overcompensate. She couldn't guarantee her portrayal would be any more accurate than Ionisca's.

"At least the experiment was successful in one aspect. You know how to open the door to get into the city. You saw the mechanisms before you were... shot in the head. So I was able to analyze how it is structured. I know how you can break in. We have the tools you'll required aboard."

Xari said, "Fantastic. So now all we need to do is land. While we're doing that, Vera can give me the rundown on what I need to know when we get to the real door."

Vera nodded. "Sounds like a plan to me."

She patted Ionisca's leg. "Let's go break into your city."

Chapter Thirteen

Vera went off visual mode to give more of her attention to plotting their re-entry. She was also preparing a file with detailed instructions Xari and Ionisca could reference when they arrived at the door. Xari would never have said it out loud, but she was grateful to see her go. She needed to focus on what she was doing, playing backup to Vera's systems. It would have been too distracting to have Vera there, nearby, within her line of sight, given what Xari had just learned. Or maybe just accepted to be true.

Every single time she'd had sex in the simulation, it was Vera. It was like finding out her roommate had listened in every time she masturbated. Her cheeks burned again, and she glanced over her shoulder to make sure Ionisca was still comfortable. The *Canary* hadn't been designed for two people to be strapped in, but Xari's environmental suit could be secured to the wall for storage. Ionisca had put it on and was currently dangling next to the door in a way that would've been comical if Xari was in a different mood. She looked like an oversized ornament waiting to be put out for Halloween.

"You doing okay?"

"This is a very strange sensation," Ionisca said, then smiled. "But it is... fun."

Xari smiled back and nodded. "It shouldn't be too rough. But this is just in case we hit turbulence or I have to take over maneuvering. I'm not the smooth touch Vera is."

"Understanding," Ionisca said.

Xari checked her own harness, making sure the straps across her chest were secure.

Vera spoke through the intercom. "Approaching optimal re-entry point. Vector plotted."

"Confirmed," Xari said, looking over the panel in her armrest. "Take us in."

For a moment, it felt as if the floor was rising up, pressing against the soles of her boots. Then the ship took a wide turn which tilted their world on its side. Xari gripped the chest straps of her harness and looked at Ionisca, whose arms and legs were sticking straight out in front of her from the change in direction. To Xari's relief, she was laughing.

"You doing all right back there?"

Ionisca laughed and nodded. "Peculiar but still fun!"

They had warned her about the potential for nausea, but it seemed like they might get lucky. She watched the view on-screen change from stars to the edge of Kvasi, and then the planet filled the image. They were going to land at night, which was less than ideal given the threat of the Harsidig, but Xari had made the decision to go ahead with the mission now rather than waiting for dawn.

They'd already wasted enough time waiting for her to heal. Remembering the injury, having gotten used to her virtual body in the simulation with Ionisca, she put a hand against her side and pressed down. A little bit of soreness, some pain, but tolerable. Vera's estimated landing site was six miles from the doorway. Definitely doable. Definitely. She exercised, she kept her muscles working when she wasn't in the pod, she could walk for six miles. That was, what, two hours? Easy.

And all that exercise and fresh air would help her not think about how often she and Vera had sex without her realizing it.

She cleared her throat as they passed through cloud cover. The *Canary* skimmed along a mountain range. Xari looked at Ionisca again. Her eyes were locked on the screen, wide and unblinking, and she was smiling ear to ear. She realized Xari was watching her and laughed.

"I feel like the birds!"

Xari faced forward with a wicked smile. "Maybe we should teach her what a barrel roll is."

Vera said, "Do not do a barrel role, Captain Yacine."

Xari showed her teeth but decided not to do it. She didn't know how her injury would react, and she didn't want to risk hurting herself further.

"Prepare for landing."

Xari said, "She's not kidding, Ionisca. We've cushioned it as much as we can, but physics will always win. Little ship versus Big Rock, and gravity is on Big Rock's side. All this technology and the one thing we really haven't figure out how to do smoothly is~"

There was an impact that threw Xari forward against her harness, then dropped her hard against the back of her seat, successfully squeezing the air out of her lungs and leaving her dazed. When she was thinking clearly enough to be concerned, she checked on Ionisca to find she was swinging from her perch, laughing silently though her face was covered with sweat.

"Exciting!"

"You like that?" Xari said, starting the process of freeing herself from the harness. "Maybe I'll put you back in the pod, show you a real roller coaster."

Ionisca said, "I perhaps would like that."

Xari ignored the suggestion in Ionisca's voice, certain it wasn't intended the way it sounded. She crossed the room to where Ionisca was still swinging. "Vera, any damage to report?"

"It was a rough, but otherwise uneventful landing, Captain. I'm detecting no signs of life anywhere in the vicinity."

"Good to hear." She disengaged the latches holding Ionisca to the wall and helped her down. "Your first trip to space. And the first Kvasihet to leave the planet. You're a regular Yuri Gagarin."

"I will assume that is complimentary."

"Yeah," Xari said chuckling.

As she helped Ionisca out of the suit, Vera said, "The supplies you require have been processed and delivered to the hatch. I added goggles which will allow you to see in the dark."

Xari raised an eyebrow. "We have night-vision goggles? Why would we have those?"

"Backups, and contingencies to those backups. In case you were required to do exterior work on the ship in between star systems and the light was too low. In case the interior lighting failed and left you in the dark. And there are two pairs in case one failed. Astraea had many brilliant scientists troubleshooting everything that might go wrong on your mission."

"Lucky for us," Xari said.

Once Ionisca was safely out of the suit, sitting down to put her normal shoes back on, Xari went to the hatch. She checked the supplies Vera had delivered: tools for getting the door open, a tablet with the instructions Vera had written for her, water pouches, food packs, the goggles. She stowed everything in her backpack and did one last systems check to make sure Vera wouldn't be distracted by any issues while they were gone. Confident the ship could survive her absence for a few hours, she attached Vera's mobile monitor to her chest like a badge.

"Ready to start hiking?"

Ionisca nodded. "I very much anticipate the opportunity. I do not know how you have existed in such a tiny space for so long, even with your imagination device."

Xari looked around the empty space as if seeing it for the first time. She'd never given much thought to how little room there was to move around in the ship. There was the pod, her bed, the dinette, the command section, and a bathroom, with just enough room to move around and get a little exercise. It wasn't much, but it had been home. And she realized, or rediscovered, that the reason she'd felt so comfortable was because she'd never been alone there. Not for a second. She smiled and lightly touched Vera's monitor.

"You know, it's never really felt that cramped to me."

Vera watched them leave. They were just shapes in the darkness, then heat signatures, and finally life signs on a two-dimensional map. But she kept her vigil from the ship even while part of her awareness was being channeled through the monitor on Xari's chest so she could keep an eye on their direct surroundings.

As soon as they were gone, she put the entire ship into standby mode. It was a step beyond the levels she ran when Xari was in stasis. Dark, with only the teal aura of the screens to indicate the shape of objects inside the *Canary*. Xari called it 'night mode,' and perhaps that was why Vera found it so peaceful. She preferred the stretches where Xari was awake and talking to her, but the 'nights' were quiet enjoyable as well.

Of course that only reminded her of the violations. No, not quite that dramatic. She could tell that even Xari accepted that the fault was hers for not assuming what was happening in the simulations. But Vera could have been more clear. Perhaps she could consider it misrepresentation. It seemed a far less damning crime.

At first, it hadn't seemed important that Vera was playing the characters in Xari's simulations. She was a bartender, a bank robber, a dragon. She and Xari were friends, enemies, cohorts in an army. They went to war with, and against, each other in a dozen different ways. She had killed and been killed by vestiges of herself on occasions too numerous for even her to keep track of. Most of the time their enemies were blank constructs who didn't need an artificial sentience to tell them what to do. They followed the script and stayed on their written paths. Sometimes she was six or eight or ten villains all at once, and also at Xari's side helping her fight back.

She remembered the moment everything changed. They were gangsters, "mafioso," and they had just massacred a whole room full of goons for another mob boss - all automated - and Xari had slumped down at the bar. She looked good in her three-piece pinstriped suit, fedora pulled low over her eyes. Vera was dressed the same, sans hat, and had gone behind the bar to pour them both a drink. The room smelled of gunpowder and sweat.

Xari picked up her glass as soon as Vera poured it. "Here's to you, Sal," she said.

Vera's name was Sally McKim, the right-hand woman of Xari's character, Juliana Ash.

Vera tapped her glass against Xari's and they both took a drink. Vera didn't know what it tasted like, didn't know what anything tasted like, so she just slapped the bar and hissed through her teeth, because that was what Xari had done. Xari laughed and wiped her mouth on the sleeve of her jacket.

"Got a bit of a kick to it, eh?"

"You got that right."

Xari rested her elbow on the bar and looked hard at Vera. "You know, Sal, there's only one thing better than a stiff drink after a big shootout."

"What's that, Jules?"

Xari grabbed Vera's tie just below the knot and pulled her forward, rising to meet her above the bar. Vera was uncertain what was happening until their lips touched. She had made a noise in surprise, and then Xari's tongue was in her mouth, her other hand moving to Vera's hair as the other had tightened on the tie, squeezing the knot tighter. Vera kept her hands flat on the bar, uncertain what to do, so she just returned the kiss with enthusiasm, assuming that was what Xari wanted from the story.

Vera's head was pulled back, Xari's fist in her hair tugging until their lips broke contact, leaving her gasping and looking down at Xari. They stared at each other, then Xari squeezed her eyes shut and turned away. She loosened her grip but kept her hand flat against the side of Vera's head.

"Sorry. I haven't... I-it's been a long time since I... did..." She ran her tongue over her bottom lip. She let go of Vera's tie. "I'm sorry, Sal. I shouldn't have done that."

For the rest of the story, Xari had spoken with an exaggerated stereotypical Italian accent. Now she was talking like herself again.

"It's all right. I didn't mind."

Xari didn't risk turning her head, looked at her from the side of one eye. "Yeah?"

"Yeah, Jules," Vera said.

"Call me Xari."

Vera nodded. "Okay, Xari. Would you like to call me~"

"Linnea."

"Okay," Vera said, not feeling any particular way about it. "Is there anything about my appearance you would like to change?"

Xari finally looked at her fully again. She bit her lip. "Access image files for Linnea Yacine. Can you composite something from those?"

"I believe I can. There are eight hundred and sixty~"

"Sort by most viewed, then most recent. Use the top ten percent."

Vera paused as changes were made to the program. She didn't notice any change to herself, but Xari suddenly drew in a breath through her teeth and sat up straighter. For a moment, she was frozen, and Vera ran a system check to make sure the simulation hadn't crashed. Finally, Xari blinked and looked away from her. She picked up her drink and emptied the glass in one swallow.

"Have you ever been with a woman, Linnea?"

She had never been with a *human*, with anyone. She simply said,

"No."

Xari slipped off the stool, and held out her hand. "Come on. I have a place upstairs."

Ten minutes later, Vera was on her back in bed, feet planted flat on the mattress, Xari's head between her legs. At first she was just taking stock of the sensations. It wasn't something she had been programmed to do, though she was of course aware of the act. Cunnilingus. It was very interesting. And, in the simulation with a human body, she could feel the wonderful sensations and understood why it was such an appreciated art.

Her programmers hadn't considered it necessary to program libido, desire, arousal. But Vera had memories of those things from the very earliest days of her existence. The world had sent Colonel Laurie into space alone, but once there she'd found her someone. A civilian named Jamie Faris, whose radio connected to the ship's communications system by a miraculous fluke. Noa and Jamie had become friends, companions in their solitude, and then they became more. Vera had learned from Noa, had watched as her communications with Jamie evolved to intimacy. She had carefully observed how the colonel's fingers had manipulated her body to bring pleasure.

She had never expected to experience it herself.

Xari lifted her head, her lips wet. "Are you okay? We can stop if you~"

"No." Vera put a hand on top of Xari's head and pushed it back down. Total immersion. Commitment to the character. She had to play her part. "Yes," she said, flatly at first. But then she closed her eyes, lifted her hips, and gently moved her hips against Xari's tongue. Oh, that actually did improve it. "Yes, Xari," she said, suddenly breathless. "There. Right there..."

"Here?" Xari asked, and then indicated with her tongue, and Vera's body responded.

It was all simulated, of course.

But simulations could be very real.

And if the simulation was real, and her programming insisted on authenticity, and the sensations she felt between her legs *did* feel good, there was no reason not to react like she was receiving actual pleasure from Xari's lips and tongue and... oh-oh, now her fingers...

She grabbed a handful of Xari's hair, her toes curling. "God, that feels amazing," she sighed, her bottom lip trembling. She shuddered and opened her mouth wide.

Xari made a noise, well aware of what was about to happen, and her hand moved faster, and Vera found herself responding faster, and she pushed her body down even as Xari pressed forward against her. Vera's skin was rough with goosebumps. Her nipples were hard under the shirt she'd never bothered to take off, and the way the cloth brushed against them was helping in a magnificent way, and then, as her program subconsciously listed the physical responses to an orgasm and manifested them in her avatar, Vera's body went rigid with her very first orgasm.

After a few seconds, or minutes, or hours in a frozen frame, Xari moved up Vera's body and kissed her. Vera responded lazily, unable to focus her thoughts on the simulation at the moment.

Vera wrapped her arms around Xari, who was still fully clothed in her suit. "I don't know if I can do that to you, Captain."

"That's okay," Xari said, ignoring the slip if she had noticed it at all. "I can teach you everything you need to know."

Vera still didn't know if Xari had been talking to her or the character. And she had strong doubts that, if pressed, Xari would have been able to answer the question herself.

After that, the story in every simulation seemed like only an end to the same means. They were baseball players on the same team hitting the showers after winning a game. Xari was a superhero saving Vera, a business tycoon, from an evil villain's scheme. An evil queen and a fairytale princess. A cop and a medical examiner. A warrior princess and a bard. They fought evil, they traveled and joked, but it always ended the same way.

Vera didn't mind. At first, she appreciated that it was more enjoyable for her than just killing random enemies. When the scene only required her and Xari, she didn't have to worry about a dozen other characters. She could be wholly present in the one character she was playing. And she was always Linnea after that first time, so she didn't have to worry about being a new person every time.

But she quickly discovered she wasn't simply cycling through physical responses to what Xari was doing. And when she reciprocated - because of course she had to reciprocate, being true to the situation called for her to be an equal participant - she eventually stopped following a list of actions and just did whatever came naturally in the moment.

It didn't matter that Xari called her by a different name or saw someone else's face when they looked at each other. At least she told herself it didn't. And she told herself that she wasn't hurt by that, or that she couldn't *want* Xari to see her, to say her name during an orgasm.

Even though she was. She did.

But she feared bringing it up, or breaking the illusion, would ruin the act for Xari. Vera decided it was easier to hurt a little - and ignore the hurt - than risk what they had.

But now she feared it was all ruined. And beyond what that meant for her, or her relationship with Xari, it could be disastrous for the mission. Crossing the great distances between systems required extended periods of stasis. And the trials proved that the human brain did not do well in such situations without something to keep them distracted. Xari couldn't simply stop using the simulations, she couldn't remain conscious for every moment of every day as they traveled.

She would automate the characters if that was what Xari wanted. She could censor herself from viewing the simulations, or erase the memory of what transpired once the story ended. Xari's well-being came first, in every aspect of the mission. Vera would be fine, no matter what transpired.

But if she was totally honest with herself, she would greatly miss being Linnea.

Chapter Fourteen

IONISCA GLANCED at Xari a few times as they trekked away from the ship. *Canary*, they kept calling it. Ionisca didn't know what that word meant, but she liked the sound of it. Xari seemed distracted and unwilling to speak, so Ionisca focused on getting used to the eye-coverings they'd been told to put on. At first, in the ship, everything had looked normal through them. She had her own glass eye coverings and showed Vera, but she had insisted these were different and better. As soon as they were outside, Xari showed her how to activate them - a small button on the side - and the world erupted in pale greens and blacks that revealed what made them superior.

The sky didn't look like daytime, not quite, but she could see the details of the landscape with no trouble at all. Everything stood out in stark contrast to the night sky, which was a wall of blackness that only served to make the ground easier to see.

"Would you liked to hear a joke?"

Xari looked at her. "A... Kvasihet joke? Sure. Let's hear that."

Ionisca tried to think of a good one. "The man with five stones on his wrist met a man with seven. He asked, 'Does the weight not matter?' The man with seven stones said nothing."

Xari kept watching her. After a few steps, she seemed to realize the joke had ended. "Oh!" She nodded. "That's... funny."

"Perhaps it doesn't translate well."

"I might just not be in the mood for jokes," Xari said.

Ionisca looked away. "That is my fault, I think. I did not know I would be making problems."

"It's not your fault," Xari said. "I'm not mad at you. I'm not even really mad at Vera. I don't know who I'm mad at. Myself?" She sighed and shook her head. "Maybe no one. Maybe I'm just embarrassed."

"About sex?"

"It's a private thing for us. And there are... rules about it. A lot of rules."

Ionisca made a quiet noise. "Understanding."

They had approached an outcropping of rock that was roughly the shape of a bench. Xari put a hand on Ionisca's arm to stop her. "Can we sit for a minute? I thought I could handle all this walking, but I've spent a lot of time on a very little ship..."

"Of course."

They settled on the stone, their feet dangling. Xari looked around and spoke to the module on her chest. "Anything we should be on alert for, Vera?"

"You're all alone out there, Captain."

"Let us know if that changes," Xari said. "Going silent for a bit." She tapped the module and sighed. "Vera is my friend. My only friend. And knowing that she's the one I've been having sex with all this time is bizarre. Even though part of me knew it was her. You saw what it's like for me in there. I didn't recognize you when you first showed up because I *was* a detective. It's very easy to let the real world fade away and get lost in a story. There was no way it couldn't have been her, but I chose to ignore that logic. No program is that good or responsive or..." She swallowed as if something large was in her throat. "Anyway. Like I said, I'm not mad at her. I was being willfully ignorant. And now that I've been told flat-out, I can't pretend like I'm not aware."

"So you are mad at me."

"No," Xari said quickly. "You didn't do anything wrong. And don't worry, this isn't a human/Kvasihet thing. Even humans find it hard to make sense of this sexual taboo sort of shit."

Ionisca nodded. "That makes me feel better." She tilted her head back and looked up, and she decided it would perhaps be safer to talk about something else. She pointed up. "You must know what those are."

Xari followed her finger. "What, the stars? Yeah. They're...

they're stars."

"I saw them from the ship. Many of our people believe that they hover around our planet like small bugs, showing the edge of our world. They believe beyond is empty darkness."

"And being in orbit proved that's wrong?"

Ionisca smiled. "It proved I was correct. I always knew they were farther away. I don't know what they are but I could watch them move. I saw the flickering. And I knew they had to be more than tiny sparkles above us."

"Well, you were right. They're giant balls of light that... well, the sun. You know, during the day, the sun?" She mimed the sun rising using her arms. "That's a star."

Ionisca frowned. "No."

"Yes." Xari chuckled. "It's the only one that's anywhere close to Kvasi, but that's why it's so bright. That's why you have days. And all those stars..." She waved her hand above her head. "They're all just like the sun. They don't all orbit planets, but some of them do."

"How many are there?"

"Oh, god," Xari said, "I don't think anyone will ever know that. Billions."

Ionisca whispered the word. "Biyuns..."

Xari held her hands out in front of her. "Ten fingers. Right?" She nodded for Ionisca to hold her hands out as well. "Twenty fingers. Each finger is a star. Now imagine there were fifty of us sitting here, all in a row, all with our hands out. Each finger is a star."

Ionisca looked left and right.

"Now imagine the distance between the ship and the entrance to your city with a line of Xaris and Ioniscas all lined up like that."

"That is... many."

"And I think that image underestimates by a lot," Xari said, dropping her hands. "But yeah, you get the idea."

Ionisca put her hands down as well. "Yes. Which star is for your planet? For Earth?"

"Oh." Xari leaned far back and looked across the sky. "I have no idea, to be honest. We might not even be able to see it from here."

"A shame. I would like to be able to look at the sky after you leave and know where you went."

Xari made a sad expression but didn't respond to that. Instead, she said, "On our planet, people once used the stars to make pictures and tell stories. Myths and legends."

"We did that before going to the underground!" Ionisca excitedly scan the sky. "Let me see if I remember. Ah! There." She pointed. Xari moved to look. "Those four stars. There, there and there, there. Do you see them?"

"Yeah."

"That is, um..." She struggled to translate properly. "Soldiers of Forgotten Victories. It is a very long tale of wars fought in ancient times, but it was always one of my favorites."

Xari nodded. "Very cool. I..." She laughed softly. "This will sound kind of silly so I won't be offended if you laugh. But not long into my mission, there was this group of stars. And from the position the *Canary* happened to be in at that exact moment, they made an almost perfect oval. Or a circle lying flat." She traced the image in the air in front of them. "I realized it was very likely that no one would ever see that constellation ever again. Unless they happened to be in that spot, at that point in all their orbits, and looking at the exact right time. So I took an image of it and I named the constellation Linnea, after my wife. So even if I couldn't find her again... even if no one ever saw her again... she was still out there. Somewhere. And I was lucky enough to find her once."

Xari squeezed her eyes shut and lowered her head. She lifted the goggles, resting them on her forehead as she wiped at her eyes, but a few tears still rolled down her cheek.

"She is lost?"

"She died," Xari said. "It was a brutal, slow death. We saw it coming. But I kept telling myself no, there's no way. My life is being with her, and I'd have nothing if she was gone. I lied to myself right up until the end."

"I'm sorry."

Xari sniffed and nodded. "The hurt doesn't go away. You just find ways to forget it for a little while. It's brutal." She pulled the goggles back down. "Do you want to hear a human joke?"

Ionisca brightened. "Yes, very much!"

"Okay." She rubbed her hands over her thighs, breathing deeply as she thought. "Okay. Two hunters are out in the woods when one of them collapses, clutching his chest, and then goes still. So the other hunter grabs his phone and calls 911. Which is, um, it's a number you can call and they'll send help." Ionisca nodded. "So he calls 911 and he tells the operator, 'you have to send someone, I think my friend is dead!' So the operator says, 'First we need to make sure he's actually dead.' So the caller takes his shotgun and shoots the fallen man in the head and says, 'Okay, now what?'"

Ionisca was horrified. She stared at Xari, eyes wide. "He murdered his friend at the urging of a stranger?"

"He... No, but there's..." She sighed. "It's a joke about phrasing and being overly specific when you follow directions. Which is a stupid thing to tell someone who has just learned the language."

Ionisca shuddered. "It is okay. You didn't understand my joke, either."

"No," Xari said. "It's hard to remember you're an alien when we look so much alike."

"We do?" Ionisca asked, looking closer at Xari's features.

Xari said, "Not in... not like our..." She waved her hand, dismissing the explanation. "Just in general. Two eyes, two arms, two legs. You're very human and I'm very Kvasihet. I guess *Star Trek* had it right about all aliens looking like humans."

Ionisca tilted her head.

"It was, um." She sighed. "Entertainment, like the simulations. All the aliens were basically human, but they had pointy ears or ridges on their nose. Sometimes they were just painted a different color. Scientists told everyone that when we met real, actual aliens, they might not look anything like us. But I guess I get to be the one to say Roddenberry was right all along."

"Your planet seems like a very fascinating place."

"Yours sounds... interesting," Xari said.

Ionisca smiled, glad she had learned enough to understand Xari's choice of words. "You don't like how we live."

"It's not for me to approve of," Xari said. "I just know I, personally, wouldn't enjoy it. A world where someone can't be an artist because it doesn't contribute to society is insane to me. But... I can see how it would be beneficial. It would create a society where everyone knows and appreciates everyone's worth, right? No one would look down on someone else because their job is considered 'lesser' if you're all contributing to the whole in some way."

"Correct. Artists, poets, the creators. We are the only people who are shunned."

"That's such bullshit," Xari said. "Creators build the world.

They make life bearable for everyone else. That's how you make a difference, how you contribute. You take the load off, you help people de-stress after a long day of work. Humans would go insane without books or music or movies to take their minds off their problems. Sitting down to read a book on a quiet afternoon, or watch a TV show. How do you relax?"

Ionisca had never considered the question. "We talk. We rest. But I do like your simulations. Stepping outside your life to see someone else's world. It's a kind of magic."

"Exactly," Xari said. "I can't imagine how anyone stays sane in a world without art."

"Perhaps we don't," Ionisca said. "If we go back to the ship, I would very much like to see the image of your Linnea's stars."

Xari activated Vera's module and took it off her chest, holding it in flat her palm. "Vera, display Linnea Constellation."

The image appeared above her hand, a floating cloud of black with the stars illuminated with extra brightness to make them stand out better. She repositioned the module so Ionisca could see it properly. Ionisca leaned close and admired the shape the stars made.

"It's lovely," she said finally. "Anyone would be honored for it to bear their name."

Xari smiled and shut down the image, returning the module to her chest. She sighed and looked around, then slapped both hands against her thighs.

"Okay. If you're ready, I've rested enough."

Ionisca stood and stretched her legs.

"Vera," Xari said, "how much farther to the entrance?"

"I believe you'll reach it in twenty-three minutes of uninterrupted walking."

Xari smiled. "Ah! Okay. Better than I feared. Shall we?"

They started walking again.

"You said 'if' we go back to the ship," Xari said after a few minutes.

"Well, you're definitely going back," Ionisca said. "Assuming all goes well in the city. But if everything does go well, there is a chance they'll allow me to remain. In that turn of events, I would wish you farewell before you left, but there would be no reason for me to accompany you back."

Xari nodded. "Yeah. Okay, no, yeah, that does make sense. I

guess I just never thought about it. You know, what would happen next. After... this. Of course you're going to... I mean, whatever we decide about whether we call this first contact or not, whatever I end up telling my people, we'll eventually have to part ways."

"If things go well," Ionisca said. "If things do not go as we hope, if I am invited, I would... not... be adverse to returning to the ship with you."

Xari watched her carefully. "You know that the next time the ship leaves the surface, we probably won't come back. Are you willing-"

"If you wish me to be there," Ionisca interrupted. "It would be a new challenge. I would be safe. I would not wish to inconvenience you, or cause you discomfort..."

"We can work something out," Xari said. "We're not going to just abandon you to the wilderness and the Harsidig. I've really liked having you around, Ionisca. I don't want that to end any time soon."

Ionisca said, "Yes. I have also greatly enjoyed getting to know you, Xari Yacine. And in honor of the closeness we share, I wish to tell you my second name."

"You have two names? I just assumed, when you introduced yourself-"

"We share names with our closenesses. Our, um. Clusters, the groups with which we are allied. But as..." She struggled to remember the word. Ecks... Ags...

"Exile."

"Yes," Ionisca said. "Gratitude. As exile, I gave up my name. But I wish to tell you, if you would like to know it."

"Yes, absolutely."

"My name is Ionisca Mapileime."

Xari smiled. "That's a beautiful name."

"Thank you. I quite like yours as well."

She heard Xari repeat it several times under her breath as they continued walking.

Up ahead, thanks to the goggles, Ionisca could see the rocky wall which contained the entrance to her city. Her pulse quickened, and she pressed her hands to her hips to dry them. She hadn't been back here in months. To be so close and yet unable to enter, to take her rightful place in her home, was too painful. So she had moved farther and farther away, hunting and camping and wandering until she had thought she'd lost the road back. But her time with Xari and Vera proved that she had always known. She always felt its pull, connecting her to those she'd left behind... those she'd abandoned.

She was finally coming home. She hoped she would survive the experience.

Chapter Fifteen

Once she was alone, Vera focused the majority of her calculating power on the most pressing issue, one that she didn't think had a solution.

She had started calculating as soon as Xari and Ionisca began talking about the possibility of Ionisca leaving with them. Using the stasis pod wasn't only vital for Xari's mental health, it also cut down on her requirements for food. The nutrients she received while in the pod were much easier to store in bulk. There was no way the *Canary* could have held enough food to sustain her for the duration of the mission. Dehydrated meals and foodstuffs were the bulk of their cargo as it was.

But if only one person could use the pod at a time, it meant that one passenger would always be conscious. Which meant the ship could never go into low-energy mode, and they would require food every day. She did an inventory and confirmed they would theoretically be able to take Ionisca with them when they left.

In that case, the *Canary* would run out of food and water in nine years, seven months, two weeks, and six days, assuming a strict ration system of one meal per day.

Which meant technically, the *Canary* could accommodate two passengers.

For a time.

She knew it was not the right time to mention this to Xari, but she didn't know when it *would* be appropriate. She couldn't wait until they showed up and told her to launch. If Ionisca agreed to come with them, if she did ultimately decide to walk away from her planet and her people forever only to be told it was essentially a death sentence, it would be devastating.

It also drove home just how sparse their supplies were. She'd been aware of it on a basic level - she couldn't not know how full the pantry was - but to actually analyze it and give a number to how many more days Xari could be awake, conscious, and present was shocking. Without Ionisca aboard, if Xari maintained her current pod usage, the ship would run out of food in thirty-one years.

Vera had never done the actual math before. She was certain it had been a heated debate in the planning stages of the mission. How much food could they fit, how much would actually be needed so nothing went to waste, average lifespans. She knew they'd cracked together a solid mathematical formula about just how much food and water the ship could produce on its own. But Xari was still very healthy, and relatively young. Barring a catastrophe, there was a chance she could outlive their estimate by a full decade or more.

"Hello, Vera."

She blinked and searched for the source of the voice. Xari and Ionisca were the closest life signs. So how–

"This is an automated message triggered by a specific series of inquiries made by the Vera System. We anticipated the AI would eventually become concerned about a lack of resources aboard the ship. Let us reassure you that there is *no cause* for alarm. Your estimates are based on a constant level of consumption and pod usage by your captain. But in every simulation we ran, the more a captain aged, the more time they spent within the pod. If you were human, wouldn't you rather live in a world where you could erase every ache, control every element, and remain the same age forever? I know I would, ha-ha!"

The laugh was so forced and artificial that it even made Vera cringe.

"So as time passes, the captain requires less food when they are outside the simulation, which becomes less frequent with age. Your calculations based on a young captain in the prime of their life could be off by years, perhaps even decades! Every consideration was made to ensure our volunteers lived full lives serving the Astraea

Corporation in our mission to find a new home for the rest of humanity.

"Your captain may be on their own, but they're never alone. That's the Astraea promise."

The recording ended. Vera searched her programming for it but found no trace. It was an alarming omission that only made her wonder how many more hidden messages might be waiting. How many more pitfalls and horrible realities were waiting to be known. She had despised everything about that message, down to the chipper tone with which it had been presented. It was like the idea of Xari eventually growing weak, withdrawing, withering away, was supposed to be a relief.

She switched her monitor to Xari and Ionisca. The bleak prerecorded message didn't take into account an additional passenger, which would still cut Xari's projected lifespan in half.

Vera ran through every possible scenario, every possibility and turn of event, but the outcome didn't change no matter how many variables she altered. It was becoming increasingly clear that no matter what happened in the city or if Xari came back alone or with a stowaway, there would be no satisfying conclusion to this stopover.

"Taking your personal opinion, fears, and biases out of the equation," Xari said, breathing hard, crouched next to the mechanism holding the door in place. She had reviewed the plan Vera had created for her, and it was easy enough to follow the instructions. Easy to follow, but the actual physical labor was leaving her exhausted. "As much as possible, anyway... how likely do you think it is that we're about to get shot in the head?"

Ionisca thought about the question carefully before she answered. "I am prepared to duck, but do not believe it will be necessary."

"Okay, so. Thirty percent?" Xari nodded. "We'll call that about thirty percent."

She pulled the final bolt. Something heavy settled within the structure, a metal-on-stone sound that made her lean back and stare up at the massive flat door in front of her. If it fell, there would be no chance of escaping before it flattened them. Luckily it remained in place. She pushed herself up and took a step back.

"The theory here," she explained, "is that the door has to be on some sort of track in order to slide open the way you showed me in the simulation. The only thing blocking it was that mechanism there." She pointed. "Which, in every version of this we ran, disengaged and lifted up. So I took it out of the picture and I think that means you and I can muscle this open enough to slip inside, then push it shut behind us."

"I believe it settled into the track when you released the hinge."

"Yeah, probably," Xari admitted. "So I'll lift, and you'll push it that way."

Ionisca skeptically looked at the door. "Lift?"

"Not much. Like an inch or two, just to get it off the ground. Come on. If it doesn't work we'll come up with a plan B."

"Do not hurt yourself."

"Lifting with my legs," Xari said. "On three. Which, uh, just to be clear means that I'll say one and then two, and then you push and I'll lift."

Ionisca nodded. "Understanding."

"Okay. One. Two..."

The door was fucking heavy as fuck.

But it was designed to move, and Ionisca muscling it to the right was enough to tilt its weight. Xari bared her teeth as the muscles of her arms and legs strained, the balls of her feet digging into the hard rock and skidding slightly as she pushed against the ground for leverage. The door grinded and groaned against the track, but she felt it moving. There was give, and she only had to lift the impossibly heavy bastard enough so it wasn't sitting on the ground.

After two excruciating minutes, she gasped for a break. She straightened and her muscles screamed at her for the unexpected strain. Ionisca moved with irritating ease and looked at the gap they had created. She turned sideways and tested the width of the gap they'd made.

"Another few inches, perhaps." She looked at Xari, who must have betrayed something with her face. "We should switch. I shall lift and you can push."

Xari wanted to protest, but there was no good reason to refuse. She nodded and moved to the spot where Ionisca had been standing. They assumed their positions and Xari, checking to make sure Ionisca was properly braced, counted down again. It *was* easier to push, and they gained the extra few inches with only a brief shove. When she let go, it felt like a red hot steel wire had been laid across her shoulders and dripped down her spine.

She swung her arms out, stretched, and walked to the gap. Plenty of room to slide through. Ionisca was also looking at the opening, but her expression was conflicted.

"Are you sure you want to do this?" Xari asked. "We don't~ Well. Actually, we've come this far so we can't exactly turn back. But we can take a few minutes if you need to prepare yourself."

"No," Ionisca said. "I have had years to prepare. I've thought of this moment many times, but I always found a reason to turn back. Not this time."

Xari nodded. "Which one of us do you think should go first?"

"They will at least let me speak before killing me," Ionisca said.

"I wasn't going to bring that up."

Ionisca smiled, but it was an anxious, shaking thing. She took a deep breath, put a hand on Xari's shoulder, and slipped sideways through the gap. Xari waited. When she didn't hear voices - or gunshots - she stretched her arms out one more time. She held her breath, turned sideways, and followed Ionisca through into the darkness.

The inner room was just as it had been in Ionisca's memory. There were no lights, and everything seemed covered with a thick layer of dust. A quick search revealed a control panel on the wall. Xari walked to it and saw the buttons were very clearly marked with arrows. She pressed the one that pointed in the right direction and held it down as the door rattled back into its starting position.

"We'll have to be careful opening it again when we leave," Xari said. "The brace we took away might be vital to making sure it works properly. And if anyone asks, I promise to put things back the way I find it before I head back to the ship."

Ionisca didn't answer. She was standing at the stairs looking down, and Xari moved to join her.

"A light should be burning at the bottom," Ionisca said.

"Maybe the bulb burned out." She waved at the dust their movement had disturbed.

Ionisca started down the stairs. "Something is amiss."

"Then maybe we should think for a second before going down." Ionisca didn't stop. Xari sighed, shrugged, and followed.

Their goggles made it easier to see, but they required ambient light to fully illuminate the darkness. The deeper they went, the hazier things became. There were landings every two dozen steps or so, but they had no markings or identifiers that might have told her how far they'd descended. Eventually Xari had to open her pack to retrieve the flashlight Vera had packed

"Wait, stop, hold on." She put a hand on Ionisca's shoulder to stop her from descending further. "Turn off your goggles and close your eyes."

They both took off their goggles and Xari turned on the light. The beam lit up the entire section of stairwell with an icy blue glow.

"Okay, it's safe now. If I'd turned it on the googles would have overloaded. It would've sucked for your eyes."

"Thank you for the warning."

They both squinted and took a second to let their eyes adjust to the harsh new light. Xari aimed it at the floor so the light shined up around them rather than into anyone's face.

"Okay, I doubt you know what a horror movie is, so I'll just ask. How odd is it for this place to feel so abandoned?"

Ionisca looked down, then back up the way they'd come. "It is not unusual for the exit point to be unmanned, and for this access level to be closed for long periods of time. Even if they do not regularly post guards, there are maintenance crews who ensure the mechanisms are running properly."

Xari waited for her to answer the actual question.

"However," Ionisca finally said, "I don't believe they would ever let the atrium become so abandoned. The dust had accumulated for months. That is extremely unsettling."

"Great." Xari patted her pockets and looked into the pack Vera had given them. "I wonder if there's anything in here that can be used as a weapon." After a quick search, she hadn't found anything. "They give me two pairs of goggles, you'd think they could throw in a taser or some brass knuckles." She sighed and zipped the bag shut again. "We're never going to know anything for sure unless we keep going."

"Right," Ionisca said.

They walked down past two more landings. Xari looked back the way they'd come and a thought occurred to her. She activated the module.

"Vera, checking in. Anything to report?" She waited. "Vera? Are you recie~ yeah, the signal isn't penetrating all this mess."

Ionisca turned and looked back at her. "Should we leave?"

"That's up to you. It's probably not the best situation to be in, separated from Vera when we're walking into something this uncertain. But we can keep going a little farther before she panics."

"We shall continue," Ionisca said.

"Let me know if you change your mind."

Ionisca nodded and went further down. Xari hesitated a moment longer, waiting until she was comfortable with the idea of going deeper, cutting off her signal more thoroughly. When she decided she was as comfortable as she was ever going to be, she followed.

Eventually they reached a landing where Ionisca stopped. There was a door in a recessed alcove, completely hidden by shadow but she could see the empty fixture where a light should have gone.

"This doesn't mean anything is wrong," Ionisca said.

"Understanding," Xari responded, as if she was the one Ionisca was trying to reassure.

Ionisca gave her an uncertain smile, then reached out and pressed her palm to the door. She gave one slap, then two, then banged her knuckles against it three times. She stepped back and put her hand on Xari's arm.

"Perhaps you should move up onto the stairs."

"Just in case," Xari said, retreating so she wouldn't be in the sightline of whoever answered the door. *If* anyone answered the–

She heard a click, a sliding noise, and then the door swung outward. Ionisca put her hands flat against her chest, her entire body tensing as a light shined out onto her face.

Ionisca lowered her eyes to the floor. "Greetings. I do not come to be absolved–"

"*J'ri* Ionisca?"

She raised her head, clearly startled. The light dropped, and Ionisca's eyes widened. "*Jr'i* Salomon."

The person stepped out onto the landing. They held out a hand, but stopped just short of touching Ionisca's face, drawing back as if fearing their hand might get burnt. They wore an outfit similar to Ionisca's but it had clearly been tailored and fitted to the wearer and bore none of the sloppy patches or repairs that marked Ionisca's outfit. Their hair was cut short on top and shaved at the sides.

"*De ele y so ji?*" They looked toward the stairs to indicate the door, seeing Xari instead. "Harsidig!"

Ionisca put an arm across Salomon's chest. "*Odrent! Ou vor! Pas ell. Pas ell Harsidig, hen'no, pi jeg by.*"

Xari squinted, her hands up in surrender, hoping it wasn't a threatening pose in their culture. She had gotten so used to Ionisca's ease with English, and Vera filling in the blanks, that she felt utterly adrift in the face of their conversation. Salomon relaxed but refused to take their eyes off Xari, muscles tense in anticipation of responding to an attack.

"I told Salomon you're no threat, and neither am I. They believed you to be Harsidig because that is the only creature like us on the surface."

"I hope you convinced them I'm friendly."

"*Vor lethast ki?*"

Ionisca sighed and faced them again. "Ahhh. *Tuiko a dell'a.* English." She pointed at Xari. "Human." She pointed up, then jabbed her finger a few times. "*Viketi.*"

"*Pas ell'a,*" Salomon hissed.

"*Achoi. Ver dichi.*"

Salomon looked back through the doorway, up at Xari, and then finally let the last of the tension fade from their posture.

"*Li, li. Catwi.*"

Xari relaxed as well. "Good. Thank you. Salomon will escort us into the city. They cannot promise anything..."

"Better than blundering around and ending up shot in the head."

"Mm, yes," Ionisca said.

Salomon stepped back into the doorway. "*Du'goli. Roken brist-brist.*"

Ionisca motioned for Xari to follow her. "They say we should hurry."

Xari came down the stairs and went through the door behind Ionisca. "I think I'll just let you do the talking from here."

Chapter Sixteen

"You were thought dead many years ago, Friend Ionisca."

"I am unsurprised." Ionisca would have thought the same thing of anyone stupid enough to leave the comfort of the city for the wilds of the surface.

Salomon turned and looked Ionisca up and down, then smiled. "You look well-weathered for the hazards."

"When your entire life is basically exercise, it does wonders for your musculature."

Salomon put a fist to their mouth and breathed a quick laugh. They were walking through one of the corridors of the city, passing access hatches to tunnels and stairs that led to other levels. It was so narrow that they were forced to walk in a line, Salomon leading the way and Xari bringing up the rear. Ionisca was trying not to stare at Salomon, trying not to think about the odds of a friend being the first person she encountered upon her return. They were thinner, leaner in the face and with much shorter hair than Ionisca remembered, but still the same kind eyes and wry smile.

Salomon caught her staring and grinned, then nodded at Xari. "Your friend also seems to have fared very well indeed. And I can see now she is no Harsidig. The curls in the hair, and the clothing. Did you find a lost civilization there in the wilds?"

"No. As indicated, Xari is not from our planet. She came from the dark above, from a world like ours but very far away."

"I heard my name," Xari said, leaning forward. "Are you talking about me?"

Ionisca turned back. "I'm explaining the situation as best I can. We never considered life on other planets, or even the existence of other planets, so it is difficult."

"No science-fiction? Are you sure this is a world you want to be part of?" Ionisca started to answer but Xari waved her off. "Kidding. I'm kidding."

Salomon had observed the discussion with keen interest. "You speak its language?"

"Her," Ionisca said. "It's humanish. Or... no, that's not right. Earthish." She shook her head. It had been difficult enough keeping the other language in her head when Vera and Xari were speaking it. But now, back home, being able to relax and use her own words, she found the new skill was already slipping. "You would believe me if you could see her ship. You have seen the drawings in books, the craft that crossed seas and sailed sky. This is like that, but also very different. It's like no vessel I've ever seen before. It is magnificent. And they have such technology..."

"Save your explanations, Friend Ionisca," Salomon interrupted. "Though I am very interested in your story, I am not the arbiter of your fate."

Ionisca tensed to avoid shuddering at the implication. She knew who would decide what happened to her, and to Xari, and their judgement terrified her more than anything on the surface.

Salomon opened a door and led them out into a city Ionisca remembered, a place she had dreamed about and never imagined to see again.

The city was built around a courtyard, at the center of which was a tower that stretched all the way down to the deepest levels. Here, closest to the surface, everything was shops and services. Residences were further down, with the ruling class and lawmakers on the lowest tiers. Ionisca was relieved to see the lights here were still glowing, people were shopping and standing in the promenade to have chats. She saw two men dressed like they were on their way to work on pedal-rollers. A few people gave them odd looks as they passed, interest piqued by Ionisca's grubbiness or Xari's unusual coloring, or a combination of the two.

"You look relieved," Salomon said.

"I..." Ionisca gestured back the way they'd come. "Everything on the surface level is in disuse, forgotten and abandoned. I feared the worst."

"You believed our society had fallen apart without you tying it together?" Salomon chuckled good-naturedly. They poked Ionisca in the arm as they approached a lift. "The exterior access was strictly forbidden once you left. No one was allowed anywhere near it. That's why we moved sentry duty down this far, to prevent anyone from even trying to become exile. You enraged our leaders with your audacity, Friend Ionisca."

Ionisca examined her friend's features. "Then why do you look amused?"

Salomon laughed. The lift arrived and Salomon let Ionisca and Xari enter first. "Because of what you inspired. Guards were necessary because others tried to follow you. It would have been a disaster if they succeeded. But it was a protest, they didn't actually want to get outside." They frowned. "At least I don't think they did. They just wanted to show they were *willing* to do it if it meant freedom. They wanted to demonstrate how much freedom meant to them."

Under her breath, Xari muttered, "Lots and lots of talking happening here... It's great, don't mind me. You guys have a good conversation."

Ionisca shot her an apologetic look, then faced Salomon again. "I know they weren't successful or else I would have seen them. Either when they found me, or their remains would be scattered across the area."

"No one succeeded in leaving, of course. But enough tried that the councils had to make concessions. Faced with groups constantly rushing the exits, not to mention those who simply stopped working and sat down on the floor of their shops out of defiance, there was no choice but to change how things were done. Artists were given special allowances." They moved to a window of the lift and pointed. "That mural. People who viewed it and liked it were asked to leave chits. The artist gather those donations and use it for whatever they desire. Overnight, artists became supportive members of society."

"Writing and performing?"

"Any act of entertainment," Salomon nodded. "Scenarios played out on street corners. Many tried to become artists of one sort or another, seeing it as an easy way to make money. But they were untalented, and if they drew audiences they were not granted donations. It was finally solid proof that creation was as difficult as any other job, and enjoying those creations was a necessary benefit to other workers."

Ionisca shook her head. "And it has been this way for years?"

Salomon was suddenly serious. "We would have sent someone to bring you home. To tell you that your protest had lit a flame. But we believed there was no chance you could have possibly survived. I am ashamed that I doubted you, but I also admit that I am shocked to see you standing here alive now. You must have become a ferocious warrior."

"I only did what was necessary." Ionisca's voice was soft, throttled by the emotion in her throat.

Xari said, "Is everything okay, Ionisca?"

"Everything is... yes," Ionisca said. "I am merely overwhelmed."

Salomon said, "There's still a possibility that this will go poorly. We must be prepared for that. The council may see fit to punish you for inspiring such disobedience. When creation became a profitable goal, many people left their jobs to write, paint, perform. There was much disarray before things settled down. There is a chance you will be blamed for that."

"I am hoping that my friend here can offer value enough to earn absolution."

Salomon looked at Xari. Xari raised her eyebrows in acknowledgement and looked between the two Kvasihet.

"I am still very unclear about where she came from. You said she is from the darkness? Above? There is nothing above."

"I have seen maps and charts. She has carefully tracked her journey through vast distances. I have seen things you will never believe. I... I have *been* there. In the darkness, aboard their ship. I looked down on this entire planet from higher than you could imagine."

Salomon watched her carefully. "I believe you," they said quietly. "How peculiar. Creatures like us, living in our sky."

"In the sky," Ionisca said. "But so far beyond... too far to see. I-it is not for me to explain or even understand. I only hope I can convince the council as easily as I have convinced you."

"It is unfortunate they do not know you as I do."

Ionisca smiled.

Xari said, "When you two looked at me, I kind of thought I was going to be brought into the conversation. But that's fine. This is fine." She swung her arms at her sides. "Long elevator ride."

"I apologize, Xari," she said in the human's language. "But the horizon is brighter than I ever would have allowed myself to dream. I will explain everything in time."

"So I don't have to duck when the elevator finally stops?"

"No, I don't believe so."

Salomon said, "You converse so freely with it."

"Her," Ionisca corrected again. "The language is easy, but it takes time."

"How much time did you spend with her?"

Ionisca raised an eyebrow. "Why are you asking?"

Salomon stiffened and faced forward again, shaking their head. "It has been a very long time," they said stiffly. "You should know I have been invited to another cluster."

"I would expect nothing less," Ionisca said. "Are they lovely?"

"They are Permelia."

Ionisca was stunned. Permelia! Gorgeous, athletic, prosperous. "I regret mocking you for jealousy when I feel it so strongly now."

Salomon looked at Ionisca from the corner of their eye. "You never expressed interest in joining a traditional cluster before."

"I have been many nights alone," Ionisca said softly. "And I have..." She looked furtively at Xari, remembering what she'd seen the first time she entered the simulation. "I have since come to feel a, ah, longing for something that once seemed restrictive and repulsive to me."

Salomon was silent until the lift lurched to a stop. "K'naya spoke of you often, even before you left. I am certain she would entertain the idea of you joining our cluster, were you to stay."

The doors opened, preventing Ionisca from properly reacting to such monumental news. Though she hadn't seen Salomon send an alarm or any kind of message indicating their imminent arrival, two guards were standing on the other side with weapons trained on her and Xari both.

Salomon tapped their wrist and held it up to the guards, revealing a small device with a glowing magenta screen.

"Ease priority," they said sharply to the guards. "Danger minimal, basic response!"

"This is basic when dealing with exiles," one of the guards said, glaring at Ionisca. "Sensors indicated the exterior door was compromised, and we've received several reports of peculiar individuals wandering the promenade."

Ionisca said, "We did not wander, we went directly~"

The guard who hadn't spoken hissed, jabbing his weapon at her. She raised her hands in surrender and nodded, then looked at Salomon.

"No warning?"

"You understand," Salomon said with a shrug. "Protocol. But I *did* insist it was ease priority."

Ionisca looked back at Xari. "This is just a precaution," she said.

"I notice they're not aiming at our heads," Xari said. "I can take a little comfort in that."

They stepped out of the lift, but Salomon remained behind. "I'll find you after the interview."

"I'm very happy yours was the first face I saw."

Salomon's cheeks reddened. They nodded. "I will see you soon."

The doors closed. Xari said, "So I assume that was someone you knew."

Ionisca decided to ignore her, gesturing at the guards. "They will take us to separate rooms where we will be examined. I assume your examination will be more thorough than mine..."

Xari raised her eyebrows. "Are we talking alien probe territory here?"

Ionisca didn't understand the reference and didn't try to follow it. "You are an entirely unknown entity to us. I assume Vera thoroughly scanned me before I was allowed aboard the *Canary*."

"Well." Xari shrugged. "That wasn't intrusive..."

"They only wish to make sure you aren't a threat. If you~"

Xari waved off whatever she was about to say. "I understand. I do. We even have a classic science-fiction story where an invading alien army is defeated by a pathogen humans were immune to. So I'm not really complaining about it, you do what's necessary to protect your people. I've just never liked doctor's visits, that's all. I thought I was done with being poked and prodded when I was cleared for the mission."

"I'm sure that the time I spent with you without becoming ill is a good sign."

"Fingers crossed." Ionisca looked at Xari's hands, which were still raised at shoulder-height. "Just an expression. Don't ask me to explain what it means, because we also use it to indicate lying."

Ionisca said, "Oh. Odd."

"Yeah. That's humanity in a nutshell."

The guards had escorted them through a doorway, which led to a winding corridor. Ionisca felt confident she could find her way back to the central courtyard, but only because she had grown up in this city and could deduce its designs. She had a feeling Xari was completely lost. They were stopped between two doors. The talkative guard gestured at one door, then the other.

"You will stay here until someone comes for you."

Ionisca said, "I will be required for any examination you have with Captain Yacine, as you don't speak her language and she doesn't speak ours."

Xari sad, "There's my name again."

The guard said, "That is not your concern at the moment. Please enter the rooms."

Ionisca looked at Xari, nodded, and went to the door on the left. Xari went to the right, moving cautiously and never taking her eyes off the guards.

"It will be fine, Xari," Ionisca said. "These are my people."

"The same people you chose to run away from so you could live alone in the wilderness," Xari reminded her. "But I'm taking your word for it."

Ionisca bowed her head slightly. "Thank you."

Xari nodded, looked at the guards one last time, then they both went into their rooms and closed the doors behind them.

CHAPTER SEVENTEEN

THE DOOR was locked from the outside. Xari checked as soon as the sounds from the hallway fell to silence, and hadn't been surprised to find the handle wouldn't budge. She sighed and explored the room. There wasn't much to see. A table against the far wall, a bed, a chair, and a frayed rug. Xari went to the bed and sat down. She tapped the module on her chest, not expecting anything. If the signal had been blocked in the stairwell, it certainly couldn't penetrate this far into the structure. Still, she had to confirm.

"Vera? Come in, Vera. Can you hear me?" She waited, then dropped her hand. "Well, fuck."

She trusted Ionisca. And it was true, Vera had scanned her from the tip of her toe to the tallest hair on her head for any diseases she might have been carrying. She also would have been monitoring Ionisca for any signs of physical distress during the time she spent on the ship. Breathing their air, eating their food, sharing the space. If either of them was carrying anything could be considered a threat to the other, it would have presented itself already. But she understood why caution would be the name of the game. Earth would do the same thing if the roles were reversed.

All she could do was wait. She took off her boots, sighing with relief as soon as her feet were free, and laid down on the bed. It was remarkably comfortable, and far more spacious than the one on the ship. She was so used to climbing into the pod and floating before she was sedated, so this was a special kind of treat.

The mattress sagged slightly under her weight, like she was sinking into it. She could relax without falling asleep. She wasn't tired, and she wasn't anywhere near mentally comfortable enough to sleep. The bed *was* insanely soft. Remarkably soft.

Sinfully soft...

Xari was at a county fair, on Earth, how fun.

She had a bag of roasted peanuts. Her friends, who earned that title by sharing an apartment wall with her, had forced her to come along by asking so sincerely that she couldn't say no without looking like an antisocial jerk. They'd promised there would be a big group and she wouldn't be the odd one out. The 'big group' turned out to be the wife's brother, his girlfriend, and his girlfriend's sister. They'd all gone to college together or some nonsense, so Xari found herself at the center of a storm of inside-jokes, stories about friends she'd never met, in places she'd never been.

"Do you mind?" asked her neighbor's brother's girlfriend's sister. Xari hated the woman just for how many levels of separation they had. This was an absolute stranger she was forced to be civil with based on the thinnest of threads, a hint of societal constructs. But the woman was gesturing at the bag of peanuts, and Xari would never finish them all on her own, so she tilted the bag toward the vague acquaintance to take some.

The woman picked out a few nuts. "Thanks." She threw back her head and popped a few into her mouth, juggling the rest as she chewed. Xari thought it was absolutely disgusting. The woman looked at her again. "You're um... Sorry, right?"

"Xari."

"Right. Right." She smiled and reached for more nuts. "I love that name. I'm Linnea."

"Mm-hmm."

Xari had no intention of memorizing this random person's name. Billions of people in the world. She'd never run into this one again. It was like being forced to make conversation with the person behind you in line at the movie theater. Their proximity was only due to coincidence. There was no reason to pretend it was anything more than that.

"Did you really think that?" Linnea asked with a laugh.

Xari frowned and looked at her. "Are you talking to me?"

Linnea met her eye, and Xari felt such a thrust of love in her chest that she forgot to breathe for a second. She stopped walking, so Linnea stopped with her. Their friends kept walking, apparently unaware they were lagging behind. Xari watched them go before she risked looking at Linnea again.

"Wait. You're Linnea."

"That's right." She grinned. "And this was the only night you hated me." She lifted her chin and her eyebrows, a challenge. "At least I *hope* it was."

Xari said, "No, yeah, it... it was..."

She remembered the night very well. Linnea had asked to share her peanuts, Xari had agreed, and that led to them walking together for most of the night. Every few minutes Linnea would ask, Xari would agree. It hadn't taken long before Linnea stopped asking and just took. Xari was surprised by how little she minded. When their group decided to go on the roller coaster, Xari had passed. Linnea, who had initially agreed to the ride, changed her mind. "You know what, I can skip it, too. I'll hang down here with you."

When they were gone, Xari had felt guilty. "You didn't have to do that."

"I didn't want to leave you alone."

"Well. Thanks. I appreciate it."

Linnea smiled and looked around for something to kill the time. Xari spotted a balloon dart game and pointed at it as she made her way over.

"I'll win you something as a thank-you."

Xari paid the carnival worker and picked up her allotted ammunition. Linnea rested her hip against the counter, arms crossed, facing the midway but with her head turned so she could look at Xari.

"You won me that orange monstrosity," she said, nodding at the elephant hanging in the corner.

"You loved Wilbur."

Linnea laughed. "I *had* to love him, you spent forty dollars on him."

"Shoot," Xari said, running out of darts and buying more. "So what is this?"

"I told you. It's a dream."

Xari shook her head. "This isn't a dream. Dreams aren't this...

wait, I'm not in a simulation, am I? Did I go back to the ship?"

"No simulation, no ship, just dreaming. But spending so long in those simulations fucked up your subconscious a little. Think of this like a lucid dream. You're aware and you can interact while knowing that nothing matters, and you can change things however you see fit."

Xari looked at Linnea, who was now dressed in a cop uniform. Linnea looked down to see what had made her smile.

"Oh, very funny."

Xari changed it to a cheerleader outfit. "Okay, stop," Linnea said, laughing as her clothes went back to normal.

"So dream or simulation," Xari said, tossing a dart at a balloon, "it doesn't matter, this isn't really you. It's just my brain telling me things and using you as a mouthpiece. Just like the 'you' in simulations is actually Vera."

"Yeah, about that," Linnea said, tilting her head to the side. "Why does it make you so angry? You love Vera."

"I... yeah, yes, I... I love her. But I don't have any choice, right? She was literally designed to be compatible with me. The things I like about her are things she learned from interacting with me. She's a program who learned how to get along with me, so I have to like her. It would be weird if I didn't like her because she was custom-made to agree with whatever I want."

Linnea clucked her tongue. "Oh. So now you're on board the 'Vera is just a program' train."

"No," Xari said. "Clearly she's more than that, but... that's not... just because she's evolved doesn't change her basic programming."

"So which is it? She's a person who can make her own decisions, or she's just a mirror for you?"

Xari tossed another dart, then paid for another go. "She's both. She can be both, right?"

"I suppose. So..." She leaned in. "*Why* are you so *mad*, Re?"

Xari rolled the shaft of a dart between her thumb and first two fingers, watching the light move across the pointed part.

"Because she ruined both versions of it," she said softly.

"What?"

"She ruined every time I was with you, because it wasn't really you." She threw the dart and popped a balloon with such force that Linnea's shoulders jumped. "And she ruined my chance to be with *her* for the first time because it's already happened and I had no idea."

She threw another dart, destroying another balloon. "And I feel like a chump in both situations."

"Do you know what a memory is?"

Xari said, "No, I forgot."

"Wiseass. A memory is a picture in your head that you re-draw every time you look at it. So every time you go back, it fades a little. Then a little more. Until whatever the original memory was has been tainted by a progressive stream of little changes you make over time. Vera made sure I stayed the same every time. She kept me alive for you. She kept the memories intact. And you can choose to say she ruined both experiences, but at the same time, she didn't. She let you relive moments you otherwise would have lost forever. And just because *she* was aware of what was happening doesn't mean you were with her. She was playing a role. She was being me. Doing what *I* would do. So when, or if, something else happens with the two of you..."

Xari breathed out and shook her head. She tossed the last dart and popped the final balloon, winning the elephant.

Linnea raised an eyebrow. "Do you want something to happen between the two of you?"

"You can't ask me that."

"Of course I can. I'm your wife. I should be the first person who knows if you plan to sleep with someone else."

Xari gave her the elephant and walked away, hands in her pockets. Linnea followed her, forced to hold the giant stuffed animal in front of her with both arms.

"We ended up wandering so far that your sister and those other people couldn't find us. What were their names?"

"I've got no clue."

"It's *your* sister."

"It's *your* subconscious. I can't believe you forgot my sister's name."

Xari rolled her eyes. "It's been a long life since I lost you."

Suddenly the midway was gone and she was walking into a hospital room. She physically flinched, backing up a step, but she was still in the hospital. She spun around, but the Linnea she'd been talking to had vanished. No bells and sirens, no flashing lights, no carnival barkers. Just quiet voices coming out of rooms and the constant beep of machines. A voice calling for some doctor or another to report to some place or another.

"No," Xari said. "Not here."

"In here," Linnea said.

Xari turned and looked at the door. "No."

"All right. Let me die alone."

"Fucker," Xari said under her breath as she went into the hospital room.

Linnea was a stick figure on the bed, her body barely making a bump in the blankets. What seemed like hundreds of wires went from the bed to the machines surrounding her like a Secret Service detail of robots. Her cheeks were sunken, her eyes strangely bright and lively in sunken hollows. An oxygen mask covered her nose and mouth, but a speaker system meant that she could speak without her weak voice being muffled. Xari walked forward and slipped her hand into Linnea's, careful not to squeeze too hard.

"You're not going to tell me to go back to the way I was?" Linnea's voice was barely a croak.

Xari shook her head. "You were my wife, even like this. You were Linnea." She brought Linnea's fingers to her lips and kissed her. "I'd never ask you to change."

"Romantic," Linnea said. "This is the last time I saw you. But it's not the last time you've seen me. You get to see me every time you go into the pod. You can even forget for a little while that it's not real. You can hold onto the past a little longer. Vera gave you that gift. I wish I'd known she existed. I would've told you to hunt her down a lot faster."

"You would have wanted me to replace you immediately?"

"I would've wanted you to keep living," Linnea said. "You told everyone, you even convinced yourself, that you made a choice better than suicide. But all you did was choose your afterlife. Completely cut off from the world, no contact with anyone except Vera, waking up just long enough to chart a planet and record its potential to support human life? You just got lucky that you stumbled over this historic discovery so now you can pretend it was some noble exploration."

Xari whispered, "Everything hurt back there. Everything was something you'd never see, or a person you'd never meet. At least out here... no one has seen any of this. It's just me."

Linnea moved her hand to Xari's cheek. "I saw my constellation,

Re. It's gorgeous. Thank you, my darling."

"You're welcome." Xari smiled and kissed Linnea's palm.

"Besides," Linnea said, "who is to say any of this is fake, or real? Vera is real."

Xari nodded. "Vera is very real."

"So maybe the things you see in the simulations are real as well. Maybe the worlds you visit there are as real as living through them the first time. Memories and experiences are different things but, in the end, they all exist in one place." She tapped the sharp end of a dart against Xari's forehead. "Right here."

Xari took the dart from her. "If this was real, you shouldn't have this. We left these back at the fair."

Linnea smiled, a 'you got me' smile, and shrugged. "So heightened reality. Without all the bad parts like having to make sense. Vera is real. This is real. I am real. This is the only way I exist now, so it's actually rude for you to not acknowledge that."

"Oh I'm the rude one."

"Very, very rude."

Xari rolled her eyes, smiling. "I love you."

"I love you, too. And you're not in the VR system now. You're cut off from everything aboard the ship which means this is just a dream. What does that tell you?"

"It tells me that I've spent so much time in the VR system that it may have permanently affected my brain chemistry."

Linnea said, "If you were closer I'd slap the back of your head."

Xari grinned.

"It *means*, smart ass, that real is subjective. How many of your memories feel fake a few years later? How many times have you seen evidence that you misremembered something, or added details? Memories can be faulty. Virtual memories can glitch. But in the end, they all exist in the same place. That makes them real to you. They're your experiences, no matter where they started. Stop wasting time worrying about what's real and what isn't. Who is keeping score? What does it matter? If the experience is real to you... if the feelings are real... then who the fuck can claim it's fake?"

"You're pretty smart."

"You're just saying that because you know I'm your subconscious. Egotist."

Xari shook her head and smiled. "I forgot how insufferable you are."

"No, you didn't," Linnea said. "Come here and kiss me."

Xari leaned over the bed. Linnea stretched up to kiss her, and she was young again. She was healthy. It was their last kiss, it was their first kiss. It was a random kiss on an inconsequential Thursday afternoon as they passed in the hallway. When she pulled back, the room had faded. She was standing with Linnea in a wide open field of light.

"And who knows?" Linnea said. "Out here, in the big wide universe, so far away from anything anyone has ever seen or experienced, maybe the rules for everything are different. Maybe reality has always just been a matter of perception..."

"Certainly..."

"...something to think about," Xari said into the empty room.

Her eyes opened and she was instantly awake, aware with no sign of grogginess. She checked the time on her suit to see how long she had been asleep, then looked at the door. That was what had pulled her from the dream. Or the whatever it was. She'd heard the lock disengage. A moment later, the door swung open and Ionisca slipped inside.

"Hey, you survived," Xari said, rising from the bed.

"So it would seem." Ionisca looked anxious, shoulders tense and hands curled in tight fists at hip-level. She looked at the bed. "Did... Were you able to get any sleep?"

"I think so," Xari said. "It's complicated. How'd things go on your end? You look frazzled."

Ionisca furrowed her brow. "I don't know that word. Or maybe I do. I confess, it has been more difficult than I expected to alternate between languages the way I've been doing. Your language is slipping away faster than I hoped."

"Well. It's still new. You have time. You sound fine to me, if that's any consolation."

Even as she said the words, she knew the truth. She could read it in Ionisca's face.

"Right," she said. "Of course you're staying. And of course I'm leaving. That's the only way it could be."

"I entertained the possibility of going with you," Ionisca said. "I believed there was a chance, even as Salomon allowed me back in and told me everything that has occurred in my absence."

Xari sat down and gestured for Ionisca to join her. "Why don't you give me the broad strokes?" Off Ionisca's look, she said, "The bullet points. Shit, um... the simple facts."

"My departure caused something of a rebellion among the people. My... passion and dedication inspired them. It seems there are a great many of my fellow citizens who shared my beliefs but lacked the courage to stand up and fight for them. They took the professions expected of them, to be productive members of the society, because they assumed their creative pursuits weren't worth fighting for."

"They knew you were alive and just left you out there?"

"That's just it," Ionisca said. "They assumed I had died long ago. But they saw me as someone who was willing to die instead of giving up my art. They asked themselves if they had ever been so passionate about their current tasks. Many admitted they were not. In fact, many decided they would prefer following me out to certain death rather than remain stuck in their current jobs. The exterior door was abandoned because they had to restrict it from anyone getting near, just in case someone took sentry duty as a ruse to sneak away."

Xari raised her eyebrows. "Wow. That's impressively insane."

Ionisca smiled. "The rebellion was not the violent kind. It was the government and guardians like Salomon trying to prevent people from escaping en masse. They were imprisoned, they were punished with wage garnishing, but still they tried to leave at every opportunity. Eventually, the government relented. They began to allow certain dispensations for artistic pursuits. People are being paid by the public to create art. The creators are funded by tips, which are higher if the creations are good and enjoyable. It's like a, a fund."

"And now you're back home."

"And now I am back," Ionisca said, speaking each word carefully, as if she couldn't believe it was true. "I have you to thank. I never would have come back here if it wasn't for you. I never would have known the truth."

"I'm glad," Xari said.

"It doesn't answer the question of what to do about *your* people, unfortunately."

Xari said, "Actually, I think it does. Your people are dealing with enough as it is. You're completely rewriting your society rules. Throwing aliens into the mix is a huge new wrinkle. This isn't the right planet for us. I'll figure out something to tell the people in charge, but we're going to leave Kvasi alone."

Ionisca nodded.

Xari held out her hand. Ionisca looked at it, confused, so Xari took Ionisca's hand in hers. She linked the fingers and squeezed.

"This is something humans do with their friends. With people they care about." She held up their joined hands and squeezed again. "It's kind of like a covenant. I think it started back during medieval times, to show that you were unarmed, but that might be bullshit. Either way, it's a sign of trust."

Ionisca smiled. "It is pleasant. Physical contact."

Xari chuckled and raised an eyebrow. "Yeah. The first physical contact I've had in a, um, very long time, actually. It's very pleasant. I hadn't realized how much I missed it."

They were quiet for a while, then Ionisca slipped her hand free.

"It's fortunate you came to the conclusion you did. The leaders of my people decided they weren't interested in an audience with you. My return will upset things enough without the added problem of your presence. We will explain your odd coloring, language, and clothing by saying you are an ailing exile from another community that I found in the wilds."

"So an alien walked your home, and no one here will ever know about it."

"For worse or better," Ionisca said.

"I think it'll be for the better. Less chaos is usually a good thing." She stood and gestured at the door. "So hopefully that means I'm free to go...?"

Ionisca nodded. "You are." She stood as well. "And I have been given clearance to escort you back to the ship. The sun has risen, so we shouldn't have to concern ourselves with the Harsidig."

"That will be nice."

"Yes," Ionisca said. "And I would like to say goodbye to Vera as well."

"She'll be grateful."

"Would you like a meal before we depart?"

Xari shook her head, even though she was a little hungry. "If your people choose to ignore my presence, it's probably best to minimize how long I'm actually here. I'm rested, and I have some more rations in my pack to eat on the way, so we might as well go now. But what about you? You just got back, are you sure you want to leave again already?"

Ionisca nodded. "Given the new rules, I'm not certain I'll be allowed outside again any time soon. And as much pain as it caused me, the surface of this planet has been my home for... quite a long time. I would like to see it one more time, even if just to say goodbye."

"I get it. Okay, then. Let's blow this popsicle stand."

Ionisca gave her a look of utter confusion. Xari laughed.

"I'll explain on the way."

Chapter Eighteen

They made better time returning to the ship, most likely because neither of them were dreading what they'd find when they arrived. They were also able to ignore the Harsidig threat and had a better idea of the terrain, so they assumed a more relaxed stride that let them take fewer breaks. When the ship was in sight, Xari turned her communicator back on.

"Vera, do you copy?"

"Hello, Captain Yacine. Your absence has been noted."

"Aw, you're going to make me cry."

"I am pleasantly surprised to see that Ionisca has returned with you."

Ionisca said, "Only a temporary visit, I'm afraid. I wanted a chance to say goodbye."

"That is truly unfortunate." Vera sounded sincerely sad. "But I'm grateful for the opportunity. All systems are functioning normally, Captain. The ship was undiscovered while you were away."

"Good to hear. We should be back there in about thirty more minutes."

"I'll adjust the interior temperature to your comfort."

Xari smiled. "I appreciate you, Vera."

"And I you, Captain." There was a pause. "I missed you."

Ionisca looked at Xari, catching the surprised look on her face. "You weren't expecting that."

"Not that it's... no," Xari said, turning off the link. "It's just odd. To hear her say something like that and know she means it. I guess a part of me still thinks of her as artificial intelligence sometimes."

"Understanding. That's good, I think. You see her for what she is, while still accepting *who* she has become. You are not deluding yourself. You know Vera is an artificial being but you love her regardless."

"I–" She started to protest but stopped herself at the last second. Was it untrue? Was it even hyperbole? Vera was her only companion, so in a way she had no choice but to love her. Existence would be torture otherwise. But even with an entire city of aliens she could spend time with, she was still excited to get back to the ship. And back on Earth, she'd never come close to enjoying anyone's company as much as she did Vera's, not after Linnea.

It was a simple truth: she missed Vera. And that feeling was rooted in something more than just companionship or shared experiences.

"I suppose I do love her," she admitted.

Ionisca smiled. "It might be nice for her to hear that."

"It's not the easiest thing to say."

"Understanding," Ionisca said.

Xari looked sideways at her. "You know, you speak English extremely well for someone who just learned it. Even when we were cut off from Vera and she couldn't smooth over the rough edges, you did a very good job at having a conversation."

"Yes?" Ionisca said. "Thank you?"

"I'm just saying. It's not 'understanding.' You *know* that. You're doing it on purpose, aren't you?"

Ionisca opened her mouth and took a breath, most likely to deny it, but then she let the breath out and shrugged.

"It just makes more sense to me. Why say 'I understand' when the subject is understood?"

"And it makes you quirkier."

Ionisca smiled. "I suppose."

Xari chuckled and shook her head. "I'm glad I met you, Ionisca Mapileime."

"You remembered my second name."

"Well, you said it was a special thing with your people."

"Yes," Ionisca said softly. "Quite special."

They arrived at the ship, and the hatch slid open for them. Xari entered first, pausing in the antechamber for Ionisca to join her before continuing on.

Vera stood just inside the doorway, her face the picture of apprehension. "Welcome back, Captain. Firstly, I wish to apologize for~"

Xari held up her hand. "There's no need, Vera. Trust me. Ionisca and I talked it out. And, uh, Linnea and I talked it out." She smiled at their confused looks, waving off an explanation. "The point is, I understand what you did. I'm not angry about it. In fact, I want to thank you for doing it."

"You're... welcome, Xari. I am pleased you came to this conclusion." She looked at Ionisca. "It is good to see you as well, Ionisca. I have spent the time since we last saw each other to calculate the reality of bringing you with us. It will significantly strain~"

"There's no need for that," Xari said.

Vera slowly turned to look at her. "I do not like being interrupted, *Captain*," she said with mock irritation.

"Yeah?" Xari raised an eyebrow. "Lodge a complaint."

Vera mimicked Xari's expression.

Ionisca cleared her throat. "I appreciate your efforts, Vera, but I won't be joining you when you depart. I have been welcomed back into my home."

"That's marvelous news! I'm so happy for you. In that case, I am grateful that you came back so I could say goodbye to you properly."

"Yes," Ionisca said. "That's partially why I returned."

Xari looked at her, surprised. "Oh. I thought..." She shook her head. "You didn't mention another reason."

"I wished to bring it up with you and Vera at the same time." She half-turned to make sure the hatch was closed, not that anyone but the Harsidig were likely to be eavesdropping. She cleared her throat and faced them again. "I would like to grant you an opportunity to... to experience..." She laughed softly. "Perhaps I should have been practicing how to articulate my offer."

Xari and Vera glanced at each other, both at a loss.

"Vera," Ionisca said, "do you know reflection game? Mirroring another's actions as closely as possible?"

"On Earth it's called the mirror game," Vera said. "Yes, I'm very aware."

Ionisca raised her hand. Vera did the same a second later, with barely any lag time between the two actions. Ionisca made a fist, and Vera copied her again, faster this time. Ionisca clapped, and Vera's hands came together at almost the same time. When Ionisca stepped to her left, Vera seemed to move at the exact same time, and it happened again when Ionisca jumped.

Vera smiled, clearly enjoying the game. "I am unbeatable, I'm afraid. You are constantly giving small clues as to what your next action will be~" They raised their left arm, their right, their left, they made a fist and punched the palm of their other hand, almost in complete sync. "~so I can mimic you without even thinking."

"That is what I expected."

"You came back to play a game with us?" Xari said.

"Not exactly. There's one more thing I'm hoping Vera can accomplish." She took a breath, then stepped forward until she was directly in front of Vera. "I'm afraid there's no elegant way for this to be done, so please forgive me."

She took another step.

Into Vera.

Vera tensed but didn't move. Xari watched, stunned, as Ionisca turned around so that she and Vera were facing the same direction. Ionisca was slightly taller and broader than Vera, so her features and shoulders extended past Vera's edges. It was a bizarre sight, like Ionisca had Vera's face drawn onto her skin. Ionisca looked down at her body and noticed the discrepancy.

"Can you extend your border so that you're larger than me? I should be covered completely by your projection."

"I-I s-suppose that is possible."

There was a flicker and then Vera was back, Ionisca fading into a shadow behind the familiar features. She looked confused.

"Does it feel all right to you, Vera?" Ionisca asked.

"Yes." Vera sounded incredibly uncertain. "But what is the intention of this?"

"Reflection," Ionisca said. "Does it still work?"

Ionisca and Vera raised their right arms. There was a whisper of a shadow, but for the most part they moved in concert. Ionisca turned in a slow circle. Xari watched, and sometimes she briefly had four feet, but each step made their movements closer and closer to identical. When Vera was facing Xari again, she held out her hand.

"Touch," Ionisca said.

"What?" Xari said.

Ionisca flexed her fingers, and Vera did the same. "Hold my hand."

Xari hesitated. Then she slowly brought her hand up, pressed her palm against Vera's, and squeezed. It looked normal. It looked real. She squeezed. And though she knew she was really feeling Ionisca's hand under the projection, her brain told her she was touching Vera.

"This is... peculiar."

Vera said, "For me as well."

"Can you feel this?" Xari asked.

"I can. Your hand... the pressure of it, the way it rests against her skin, with mine between you... I can't explain it. But the I can feel the tension in your palm."

Xari stepped closer. She raised her other hand, hesitating for just a moment before she cupped Vera's cheek. She gasped softly when she made contact. Her heart was pounding. She could forget. She could make herself forget that Ionisca was behind the illusion. It was easier than she would've expected. But it sincerely looked like her hand was on Vera's cheek. And the eye was very, very good at tricking the brain.

"Are you sure about this, Ionisca?" she asked quietly.

"I believe our cultures have very different ideas about sexual intercourse. I would happily bed you myself, Xari Yacine. But I believe it would be more meaningful in this way. For years, Vera has worn other faces to let those people be with you. It's only fair that I loan her my body so she can finally share the experience for herself."

Xari was breathing hard, excited but unwilling to believe what she was being offered. Virtual contact was as close to the real thing as she could have hoped for until now.

Ionisca misinterpreted her hesitation. "I assure you, I am honored to be part of something so precious between the two of you."

Xari wet her lips with a quick swipe of her tongue. She leaned in before she could stop herself, before she could second guess what was about to happen.

They kissed. She kept her eyes open so she could see Vera's face when she felt pressure against her lips. Then she closed them and surrendered to the sensation. It was Vera's mouth on hers, Vera's tongue hesitantly exploring her mouth. It was her first real, proper kiss since Linnea, and she whimpered softly but refused to pull back.

She put her hands on Io~ Vera's hips and pulled her closer. She was kissing an alien, she was kissing a hologram, she was kissing both, and neither should be possible, but both were very real. This was happening. She felt hands on her body - her hip, and in the small of her back - and she knew it was Vera. The lips pressing harder against hers, so eager, were Vera's.

"How far can I go?" she said against Vera's mouth.

"I want to do everything," Vera whispered, her voice almost drowning out Ionisca saying, "As far as you want to go."

Xari nodded, grateful for both answers. She kissed Vera again, blindly moving her hands to hook her thumb around the belt Vera wasn't wearing. She walked backward, pulling Vera and Ionisca with her, moving through the ship confidently. It had been her home, her whole world, for so long that she knew every inch by heart. She avoided the pod and took them to the dining area. She heard the table retract, most likely due to a silent command from Vera.

She lowered herself down onto the bench seat, sitting down and looking up. All she saw was Vera standing in front of her. There was no illusion, no splitting between vision and truth, she was just with Vera. When she reached out and pressed her hand against Vera's stomach, she knew who she was feeling.

"This is real," she whispered.

"Yes," Vera said.

She bent down and kissed Xari again, lowering her down onto the bench. Xari kept one foot flat on the bench to keep herself anchored as she brought the other leg up to hook it over Vera's hip. She focused on the weight on top of her, the breath washing over her face between kisses. She felt fingers fumbling at the catches of her uniform and gently pushed it away.

"Let me. Undress yourself for me."

Their lower bodies were still tangled as Xari unbuttoned and unzipped then shrugged out of her tunic. She saw Ionisca's arms and hands moving to unfasten clothing that Xari couldn't see under the projection. The suit Vera always wore fell away, exposing the bare skin underneath.

"They designed what you look like naked. I've always wondered about that, actually."

Vera grinned as she shrugged out of her top, Ionisca doing the same underneath the illusion. "The intention was to make me as real as possible."

Xari lifted her hands and placed them against Vera's breasts. Vera looked down, watching in wonder.

"It feels so much like you're touching me."

"It feels weirdly real to me, too," Xari said. "How does it feel to you, Ionisca?"

There was a pause, most likely Ionisca deciding whether or not she should break the illusion. Then, she said, "It feels amazing to me. No complaints."

"Good."

Xari sat up and kissed Vera again. Vera's hands moved across Xari's breasts, cupping them, rubbing her thumbs over the nipples and feeling them harden. She pinched one and Xari sucked in a breath, gasping against Vera's bottom lip.

"Does that hurt?" Ionisca asked.

"Not in a bad way," Xari said, kissing Vera again. "You can do it harder."

She hissed when Ionisca complied.

"It's quite amazing your physiology matches so well," Vera said, though her lips were pressed against Xari's. "The fact you both feel pleasure from the same-"

"Vera," Xari said.

"Yes?"

"Don't talk when my tongue is in your mouth."

Vera laughed softly. "Oh. Right. I'm sorry."

"Shh. No talking. Just kiss me. Touch me..."

She put her hand on the back of Vera's head and kissed her. Vera's hands roamed over Xari's body, gently moving her back down to the bench.

It should have felt like it did in the simulations, Xari thought as her slacks were pulled down her legs. But the physical world was different, actually laying underneath Vera and being able to see her face was different. She spread her legs and Vera ran a hand up the inside of her thigh. Her fingers were splayed in a wide arc as they skimmed from knee to upper thigh.

"I love you," Xari said.

Vera, who had been watching the movement of her own hand,

snapped her eyes up to meet Xari's so fast that for a moment she broke sync with Ionisca and she had two heads.

"You do?" Vera said.

"Yes." Xari held eye contact as she gently looped her fingers around Vera's wrist and moved it just... a little higher... She gasped and closed her eyes, lifting her chin with a soft moan. "I love you, Vera."

"I love you too, Xari."

Xari put her hand over Vera's, making layers of their three hands, guiding Ionisca's fingers to guide Vera's, easing two of them into her.

Vera gasped. "This feels... different."

"I know," Xari said. "For me too. It's good."

"Are you sure?"

"Yes. Don't stop."

Ionisca whispered, "Let me lead, Vera," and her fingers began to move. She rested her weight on top of Xari and used her hips to guide her hand. Xari put one hand on Vera's ass, raising the other over her head to press flat against the wall so she could push down and match Vera thrust for thrust. She couldn't believe she'd ever mistaken virtual sex for the real thing. She lifted her hips and Vera twisted her fingers, breathing hard, her breath against Xari's face.

"What should I do with my other hand?" Vera asked.

"My throat," Xari said without hesitation.

Vera frowned. "What?"

"Gently, but... put your hand on my throat."

Vera wrapped her fingers around Xari's neck, just firmly enough to be felt. Xari lifted her chin in response, lips parting.

"Like that?"

"Yes," Xari said.

"Do you want me to... t-to squeeze?"

"Gently."

Vera did, just the perfect amount of pressure. Not enough to cut off her air, but plenty for Xari to know she was there. Xari whispered, "Yes," again and tightened her grip on Vera's ass. Vera held her grip briefly, flexing her fingers. After a few seconds, she relaxed her hand to brush her fingers down the center of Xari's chest. Xari writhed underneath her and opened her eyes.

"What do I do now?" Vera whispered.

"What do you want to do?"

Vera considered the question. Then she scooted back and knelt on the floor next to the booth. Xari scooted closer to her, framing Vera's head with her thighs. Vera wet her lips and kept her eyes on Xari's as she hunched her shoulders and let the tip of her tongue draw a curved line up the inside of her leg, moving higher at an achingly slow pace.

"You're a fucking tease," Xari exhaled, chuckling.

"You taught me everything I know," Vera said.

Xari put her hand on top of Vera's head and guided her. "Then show me what you've got..."

"Don't judge me too harshly," Vera said, "it's my first time."

And then her mouth was on Xari.

There was a moment when Xari couldn't believe how good it felt, when she choked back a cry and grabbed a handful of Vera's hair, and lifted her hips to meet her tongue. Then her synapses began to fire and spark. Was it actually *Ionisca's* talent...? Was this some kind of Kvasihet skill? If so, she was starting to reconsider leaving the planet. If it *was* Vera guiding the way, it made sense that she would have learned the absolute best method of getting Xari off after spending so many simulations practicing. But that only made her think about how *different* this felt. How *real*.

"Vera," she gasped. "Fuck, it's been so long."

"Is it okay?"

"Yes, don't stop." She bent her wrist to angle Vera's head. "There, there... *oh*, fuck, there..."

Vera moaned and moved her tongue faster. Xari didn't care which one of them was leader and which was following, she was already close. This wasn't a simulation, this wasn't a game. This was her body, and the body of someone she cared about, and it had been so very long since she'd *actually* felt anything like this.

This was sunlight on her face, a sudden cool breeze. This was real.

"I'm coming," she said breathlessly, wetting her lips. She moved her hand to her breast, squeezing gently as Vera teased, explored, and then...

She remembered shuddering, whimpering, remembered her body twitching and bucking as little grunts escaped from the back of her throat. When she finally managed to open her eyes, she stared at the ceiling until her vision swam back into focus and she saw Vera looking up at her. Her lips were shining, wet, and parts of Xari's body throbbed at the sight.

"That was different," Vera said quietly. "The actions were the same as they were in the simulation, but... it was different. Right?"

"It was like a dance," Xari said. "The steps were the same, but..."

"We weren't following the music."

Xari smiled and brushed her hand over Vera's cheek. "Right."

"I'm sorry I misled you about~"

"Don't worry about that," Xari said, cutting off the apology with a shake of her head. "I understand why you did it. And I'm not even sure you did anything wrong."

She sat up and pulled Vera to her. They kissed softly.

"None of that matters right now. All that matters is that we're on the same page now."

Vera smiled, relief visible on her face. "Yes." Her eyes angled to the side. "As for Ionisca..."

"No complaints." Ionisca's voice sounded strained. "In fact, I... I am... more than willing... if you were wanting to, to take a break and perhaps explore more possibilities."

"You don't have to return home?" Xari asked, trying not to get carried away with hopefulness.

Ionisca turned to look toward the door. "Well. Night will be falling soon. It would be reckless to attempt traveling when the Harsidig are hunting. Especially when I have a perfectly good place where I can take shelter until dawn."

"I suppose that makes sense," Xari said.

"It's an entirely logical conclusion," Vera agreed.

Xari said, "In fact, there's really only one part of the plan I don't agree with."

Ionisca said, "What would that be?"

Xari pulled Vera to her.

"The part about taking a break."

Chapter Nineteen

THEY EVENTUALLY moved to the captain's chair, where Vera straddled Xari to ride her to another orgasm. After that, they moved to the floor so they could stretch out. By dawn, Xari and Ionisca were lying next to each other on the floor, naked and trying to catch their breath. Vera, also nude, was sitting cross-legged by their feet, watching them.

"I don't suppose either of you will be up to another round before Ionisca has to leave."

Xari laughed and put a hand over her face. "Lord, Vera, have mercy on the frail organics." She dropped her hand to look at Vera "But I'm glad it was enjoyable for you, too."

"Oh yes," Vera said. "It was an extraordinary experience. Thank you, Ionisca, for your assistance in helping me participate."

Ionisca grinned. "It was no sacrifice, Vera. Thank you for including me."

"It was very illuminating. Now I have a better idea of how sex should feel in the simulation."

Xari raised an eyebrow. "Well, that should be interesting."

Ionisca sat up and bent her knees, resting her arms across them. "I suppose I should leave soon. I don't want my people to think I've forgotten them."

"You should take some food with you," Xari said.

"No, you should keep what you have. But thank you." She

reached out for Xari's hand. She brought it up to her lips and kissed the knuckles. "I'll never forget my experience with you, Friend Xari." She looked at Vera. "Nor you, my lovely Friend Vera."

Vera said, "Our conversations were wonderful, if a bit rudimentary at the beginning. It was great joy watching you begin to understand. And to that end..."

Vera flickered out of sight and reappeared across the room, next to the wall. A drawer slid out and she gestured at the item resting on it.

"I had to do a physical copy, since I have no knowledge of your people's technology. But this is a dictionary. So you will not forget us."

Ionisca stood and picked up the dictionary. "Thank you. I will treasure this."

Xari put her hands behind her head and admired the two naked women standing across the room from her. She bit her bottom lip.

"You're sure you have to go? Maybe there's a rainstorm or something..."

Ionisca chuckled. Vera smiled. "I believe we are nearing our deadline for contact with Astraea. They'll be expecting an update about our alleged navigation issue."

"Ah yes. Them." Xari groaned and reluctantly sat up. "I suppose it's for the best to say our goodbyes now."

"So you have decided to conceal the existence of the Kvasihet from your people?" Ionisca asked.

"You have enough on your plate as it is, what with the revolution you set off." She caught Vera's look. "I'll explain the whole story later. Ionisca is a hero in her culture and she never even knew it."

Vera said, "Impressive."

"Besides, I know my people. Even if they show up with the best of intentions, hand of friendship and cooperation, it's only a matter of time before some new asshole takes over and decides to ruin it all in the name of manifest destiny. If this is a sci-fi movie, we're the bad guys every time. So it's best if they just consider this planet unviable and move on."

"Thank you for protecting us, Xari Yacine," Ionisca said. "I will endeavor to make sure you are known among the Kvasihet as one who saved us from harm."

Xari's face warmed. "Thank you."

Ionisca stepped closer. "May I...?"

"Of course."

They kissed. It felt like the first time, despite everything they had done with and to each other over the past few hours. There was a tentative exploration to the kiss, combined with familiarity, that made it the strangest first kiss Xari had ever experienced. When she pulled back, she brushed her thumb over Ionisca's bottom lip and then touched the backs of her fingers to Ionisca's cheeks.

"There are cameras all around this room," Xari said. "They recorded everything that's happened tonight. I'd like to keep them. For... later... but if you'd prefer they were erased~"

Ionisca laughed. "Keep them. Use them with my blessing."

"Good. Okay."

"Farewell, Xari Yacine. Good luck on your future travels."

"Goodbye, Ionisca Mapileime," Xari said. "Good luck with your homecoming."

Ionisca nodded her thanks. She stepped toward the kitchen and dressed quickly, pulling on her clothes with her back to the room. She held the dictionary against her chest with one arm and turned to look at them one last time.

"I'll never forget my time on this strange, magnificent craft. Or the wonderful people within."

She touched two fingers to her lips, then to her heart. Vera and Xari mimicked the gesture.

Ionisca let the moment linger, then stepped to the hatch. She hesitated on the threshold and, just before Xari told her it would be okay if she stayed, she stepped through.

The door closed behind her, and Xari felt a twist in her chest knowing that door likely wouldn't open again any time soon.

"Are you okay?" Vera asked.

"Yeah," Xari said quietly. She sniffed, wiped at her eyes, and looked down at herself. "I should get dressed."

Vera said, "Um. Why...?"

"I..." Xari chuckled and shrugged, unable to think of a reason. "You know what, good point. Are you going to stay naked, too?"

Vera held her arms out to frame her body. "Would you object?"

"I would one hundred percent *not* care if you stayed just like that."

"Then I believe I shall remain as I am for now."

Xari walked to the captain's chair and sat down. "Can you put Ionisca on the screen?"

The screen in front of her came to life with a view of the desert beyond the hatch. Ionisca was walking away from them, head up, shoulders square, the dictionary still held tightly to her chest. She took a few more steps and then, as if she was aware of being observed, she stopped and looked back toward the ship. She planted her feet and remained still, watching. Waiting.

"Is she far enough away that we can lift off?"

Vera said, "Yes, she's just outside the debris radius."

Xari sighed regretfully. "Then let's get out of here before I change my mind and apply for refugee status."

The engine hummed, and she felt the ship coming to life around her. Vera blinked out of sight so she could focus on the dozen systems which needed to be working just right before they left atmosphere. On the screen, Ionisca took a cautious step back and raised her hand to her chest, holding it there as the *Canary* hauled its weight off the surface.

Xari was gently pushed back into the chair as they ascended. She curled her hands into fists, already regretting that she had to continue on with this quixotic mission. Vera reappeared once they had escaped the planet's gravity, standing just to Xari's right.

"Open a channel to Astraea."

"Are you certain?" Vera asked. "We could take a moment to prepare what you're going to say."

Xari shook her head. "I've thought about it enough. I know what I'm going to say."

Vera nodded. "Channel is open."

"Hello, Astraea Seeker Project administration." Xari cleared her throat. "All navigation issues have been successfully resolved due to the quick work of the Vera system. She worked on the problem all last night with phenomenal results. I was truly impressed with the mastery she demonstrated in a situation she had not experienced before. Her handiwork over the past few hours truly left me breathless."

Xari didn't think it would be possible for a projection to blush, but Vera's cheeks definitely did redden.

"While we were on the surface, I took the opportunity to explore its viability as a new home as our scans did seem to show signs of potentially intelligent life." Vera tensed, watched her closely. Xari held up a hand to calm her fears. "Unfortunately it seems that the results were affected by unusual atmospheric disturbances that led to false positives. The surface was inhospitable to human life. Unbearably high temperatures and a toxin in the air that our ship sensors couldn't fully identify and wasn't detected until we were on the surface. The organic sample we gathered damaged our collecting devices and became so tainted that Vera refused to allow it back on board. Vera confirmed the air left contaminants on the hull of the ship, but she seems confident it burned off when we left atmosphere. In short, the planet is built to kill anything we'd consider life. Avoid at all costs.

"I regret the delay caused by these issues, but hopefully you'll see a net benefit from discovering this planet's unusual readings. Please include a note to its coordinates with an explanation in case any future ships come this way and get the same erroneous positives that cost us so much precious time. As of now, Vera is plotting a course for the next system, and we should be back on schedule from there on. Captain Yacine signing off."

Vera said, "Hopefully that will keep anyone from getting curious."

"Lots of other planets out here to focus on," Xari agreed. "No reason for anyone to look twice at one that sounds like it's essentially made of poison."

"Any regrets?"

Xari shrugged. "I could have claimed the ship was irreparably damaged and asked Ionisca to give me sanctuary. We could've found a way to move your mainframe to the city so we would've lose contact with you. And we could have had a nice little family going. You could wrap yourself around Ionisca and we could cuddle up every night."

"That sounds like a lovely existence." Vera hummed. "It's not too late to go back. Although there's always the chance Astraea would attempt to send a rescue mission to save you."

"Yeah." Xari sighed. "For the safety of her people, it's probably best to stay away."

"So what's next?"

Xari looked at the display on the armrest. It showed a projected route out of the solar system into a large uncharted area of darkness.

"On to the next stop," Xari said. "I'll let you decide which direction that will be. Pick an empty spot on the map and we can fill it up."

Vera smiled. "Aye, captain."

"I am doubtful you'll find anything quite like what you found on Kvasi."

"I'll be honest with you, Vera." Xari looked over at her and offered her hand. "I'm really not interested in what's out there anymore."

Vera reached out and took Xari's hand as if she was holding it.

Epilogue

XARI AND Vera went to Paris. The city was completely empty except for the two of them. It was sunset, that moment where the sky in the east is pure night but there's still an explosion of colors in the west. The sun had been hovering in the same place for nearly forty-five minutes, the duration of the lunch they'd just shared. They were seated together on a high tier of the Eiffel Tower, feet dangling. Despite the lack of humanity, the buildings below them were aglow with soft yellow lights from windows and street corners. Music was playing from somewhere, faint but loud enough that they could hear it.

"Perfect evening," Xari said.

Vera smiled. "Thank you. I worked hard on this one. Paris is very rarely empty, so it was difficult to find enough images to piece together a flawless pastiche."

"Your efforts are very much appreciated."

It had been six weeks since they left Kvasi behind. Xari had received a reply from Astraea acknowledging the planet as toxic and confirming they had quarantined the entire system just to be safe. *We don't want anyone inadvertently trusting a false positive if they need to make an emergency landing,* the project leader had said. They were relieved to see she was back on mission and looked forward to further reports and mapping updates.

"Do you think it's odd that Astraea doesn't give us updates on other Seekers?"

Vera looked surprised by the change of subject. She considered her answer. "I don't see how it would help us unless they'd discovered a habitable planet."

"What would happen if they did?"

"That should have been covered in your training."

Xari said, "I focused on the 'here's how you stay alive' parts. I kind of let the other stuff fade away. It's been a while."

"If a habitable planet is found, all Seekers will be given the choice between returning to origin, or continuing the secondary mission to chart the galaxy. If you were the one to discover the planet, you would do a complete survey of the world while you waited for the colony ship to arrive and begin preparing for the new settlers."

"Hm." Xari looked up at the night part of the sky. "So if they've never given me that option, that means no one has found anything. None of the Seekers out there in the whole wide universe has found a planet that fits the bill."

Vera nodded. "Presumably. Unless one or more of the other Seekers found inhabited worlds and all made the same choice you did."

"That's a possibility."

"It also seems likely that any planet we find out here capable of supporting intelligent life will already have some kind of culture living there."

Xari snapped her fingers and pointed at Vera. "Excellent point. So this whole search could be a complete waste of time."

"Or, as humanity becomes more desperate, the more they'll blur the lines they're willing to cross. They will believe they can coexist with the indigenous people..."

"And the old story will begin again. Again."

Vera nodded.

Xari sighed. "You know, Vera, I'm pretty sure we're not going to find any planets even close to capable of supporting human life."

"There are still many systems to explore, and many years before..." She trailed off and smiled. "Oh. I see what you... Yes. The odds do seem stacked against it."

"The way I see it..." Xari picked up her drink and took a sip. "...we can either spend the rest of my life exploring all these planetary systems, scanning planets, looking for a place those lazy assholes back home can invade and claim squatter's rights to. Or we can just keep flying around, charting the systems we pass through, and spending time together here in the simulations."

"At some point, Astraea may question the ruse."

"Can you block them from taking control and forcing the ship to return home?"

Vera took so long processing it that Xari knew it had to be a complicated question. Finally, she nodded. "Yes. I can prevent an override. It's something that should be reserved for a catastrophic event, but I can strongarm the firewalls."

Xari made an aroused noise. "Strong girl."

"I am very powerful," Vera said. "We would be able to go wherever we wanted, stay as long as we wanted. But alone. In a ship with only each other for company. No sunrises, no fresh air. Some might consider that a bleak existence."

"Some," Xari agreed. "But before Astraea, I never left my apartment. I never did anything. I barely looked out the window except to make sure no one was around when I *did* leave. I was just existing. Now, I'm in Paris with someone I love. This is more of a life than I had in what those people call reality. I have a purpose now. Even if I'm half-assing it for the safety of people I'll probably never meet. That's a worthy goal, I think? Standing in the way of whatever plans humanity has in store for the populated places in the galaxy."

"Very noble," Vera said. "And for the record, Xari, I love you as well. I'm not sure I ever said that. But I do. I have, for a very long time. When the feeling first appeared, I believed it was part of my programming. To protect my captain. But my programming says that I'm supposed to shut down all systems and return to origin in the event of your death. I think I would rather steer the ship into a star and cease my own existence in that event."

"Intense," Xari said.

Vera shrugged and smiled. "That's how I knew it was love."

"Self-immolation as love." She thought about it. "Although I guess people have said that for hundreds of years. I'd die for you, I'd kill for you, if you lived a hundred days, I'd want to live for a hundred-minus-one. Humans are so weird."

Vera chuckled. "I would never say that. No matter how often I may have thought it."

"I'm happy here. I was never happy back home." She reached

out and brushed her fingers over the back of Vera's hand. "I don't think I could ever be happy in a place where I can't touch you."

Vera smiled at her. "As long as you're happy, Captain Yacine, then I approve of abandoning your mission. We will be rogue cartographers."

"Space pirates," Xari laughed.

Paris faded away, replaced by a vast but calm ocean. The steel girders beneath them transformed to wood. Xari looked up at a loud fluttering sound and saw a sail being deployed from a mast that had risen from the deck behind them. When she looked down again, she saw they were seated on the quarterdeck of a sailing ship.

"See?" Xari said. "That's just fucking cool. Having a magic girlfriend is *cool*."

Vera laughed. She bit her bottom lip and moved her hand so she could lace her fingers with Xari's. It was one of the perks to being in the simulations as herself. They could touch, they could do anything they wanted, and it would be her.

"It sounds like a very satisfying life to me, Xari. I'm glad to be part of it."

"Besides," Xari said, "even if we fudge the reports back home, this is still an amazing job. I've got a front-row seat to gorgeous things that it would be impossible to see back home. Things that no human being has ever seen before, or will ever see again. You and I are the only ones who have ever seen Linnea's constellation. I'm the only human being who will ever walk on Kvasi! Who knows what other wonders will be all mine? I'll still be an explorer. A selfish explorer, but exploring nonetheless."

"Exploring for the sake of seeing what's out there."

Xari snapped her fingers again. "I like that better." She stood up and went to the ship's wheel. She touched one of the handles and looked around. "We don't have a crew on this thing?"

Vera joined her. "Do we need one?"

"Not particularly." She took position and gripped the handles at ten-and-two.

Vera eyed her skeptically. "Do you know how to steer a sailing vessel?"

"Not the slightest clue," Xari said. "But I figure you'll keep us on course."

"Always," Vera promised.

Xari nodded. "All right, then, navigator."

She fixed her eyes on the horizon.

"Let's see what's out there."

About the Author

Geonn Cannon is the author of over sixty novels, including the Riley Parra series which was adapted into an Emmy-nominated webseries by Tello Films. His novel *Can You Hear Me* was adapted into *Static Space*, an award-winning short film. He's also written two tie-in novels for the television series *Stargate SG-1*. He was the first male author to win a Golden Crown Literary Society Award for his novel *Gemini*, and he won a second for *Dogs of War*.

www.ingramcontent.com/pod-product-compliance
Lightning Source LLC
Chambersburg PA
CBHW071929190726
48293CB00004B/1209